The Mystery of
BLACKBEARD THE PIRATE

CAROLE MARSH MYSTERIES™

Written and Photographed
by Carole Marsh

Reading up on Blackbeard

The Kids and Blackbeard's "missing" head

MEETING BLACKBEARD!

An author's favorite book is often her first—and that's true for me! My kids were ages 7 and 14 when they first begged me to write a mystery book for them. I did! It was called "The Missing Head Mystery"—today updated and retitled "The Mystery of Blackbeard the Pirate."

Michele and Michael and I had just started visiting the tiny town of Bath, North Carolina. Why? Because it was the closest place to our home that was on the water. We stayed in a little motel on Bath Creek that had only four rooms. But there were sailboats, and paddle boats, and barbecue pits, and pirates!

Bath, the oldest town in North Carolina, was once the home and haunt of the fiercest pirate of them all—Blackbeard! I actually met Blackbeard one night. I was walking down the street and came toe-to-toe with a big pair of black boots. Slowly I looked up to see big, baggy black pants, then a big black coat covered with pistols and cutlasses. In fear and trembling, I raised my head to come face to face with a man with a big, bushy black beard tied up in tiny red bows. He also wore a large pirate hat complete with feather and had matches stuck behind his ears.

He said, "Hi!" An actor in the local outdoor drama, he told me all about Blackbeard and his life as a pirate up and down the east coast of America. This, I thought, would make a great mystery! My kids thought so too and helped me by finding every secret passage and tombstone in town. How we ended up with Blackbeard's head is another story, but I guess you don't want to hear about that, hey? You'd rather get started reading this mystery!

Carole Marsh
Pirate Fan

Dedicated to the "real" Michele and Michael, my now grown up kids, and Brian and Jo Dee.

| Michele | Michael | Brian | Jo Dee |

ABOUT THE CHARACTERS

Michele is the author's daughter. She was 14 at the time this book was written. Today, she is president of Gallopade International, which publishes her mother's mystery books, and, is the mother of Christina and Grant, who appear in many Carole Marsh Mysteries.

Michael is the author's son. He was 7 when this book was written. He was the "keeper" of the ugly prop head of Blackbeard the pirate, and enjoyed playing many practical jokes with it. Today he is vice president at Gallopade International, responsible for new product development. The "head" hangs in his office!

Jo Dee grew up in Bath and actually lived in the house where the Blackbeard's Treasure gift shop is located.

Brian is also from Bath and played football on the Bath Pirates team.

Carole Marsh and her family lived in Bath for many years – right next door to the Buzzard Inn.

Titles in the Real Kids Real Places Series

Books and Teacher's Guides are available at booksellers, libraries, school supply stores, museums, and many other locations!

For a complete selection of great Carole Marsh Mysteries, visit www.carolemarshmysteries.com!

CONTENTS

1 A Stolen Head

"His head is missing?" Mother asked with a laugh.

Michele, who was pecking out her name - Michele Hunt, age twelve - on the computer in the breakfast room, paused to listen to her mother's strange phone call.

"Oh, I'm sorry," her mother said, now with a serious tone in her voice. "I didn't realize the loss of the head could mean such a terrible tragedy."

Michele listened intently now. What in the world could Mother be talking about, she wondered.

Her brother, Michael, sneaked into the living room through the side door. Michele guessed he didn't want Mother to see that he was soaked with soap and water from washing the car. He was a little short to be seven and had to climb all over the sudsy car to reach the top.

Tiptoeing into the breakfast room, he mouthed a "Where's Mom?"

Yuck, Michele grimaced, even his mouth was foamy. She whispered "Shhh," and pointed to the computer monitor for Michael to watch. She began to type slowly in the rhythmic pace Mother said would help increase her speed. She had started typing lessons as soon as school was out so she would be ready for the drama club she wanted so badly to be in next year. She thought that if she were able to type scripts, it might help her get accepted.

She had seen a Broadway show when she went with her Mother to New York City to see a publisher. Ever since, she'd been hooked on the theater. It just seemed to offer something for everyone, no matter what your talents.

Michael leaned over Michele's shoulder and watched as she typed:

"His head is missing . . ."

He squiggled his nose and squinted his eyes like he always did when he didn't understand something but didn't want to admit it.

Mother came around the corner to the breakfast room. She stretched the phone cord and sat down on the bench across the table from them, still listening carefully to the caller.

She smiled at Michael and Michele and gave them that loving once-over Michele knew so well. She would always stare at their pale blonde hair, then look them both deep in their blue eyes and round faces, like she was looking into a mirror back in time, perhaps when she was their age.

The three of them looked so much alike it was incredible. People would always comment about it when they went anywhere together. Even their bald-headed baby pictures all looked alike. The comments always made Michele feel a little self-conscious, and Michael always scrooched up his face.

Mother shook her head slowly. "Now I'm not really sure I want the kids to come down," she said to the caller. "It may not be safe."

She handed the receiver to Michael to hang back up, then stared blankly out the window. "Bath," she said absent-mindedly.

"Mom," moaned Michael, slapping his arms against his sides with a squish-splat. "I can't get much cleaner than this."

Mother looked at him and laughed. "If the car's as clean as you are, you've earned your three bucks," she said. "But I don't mean tub bath. I mean Bath — Bath, North Carolina."

Sometimes Mother didn't seem to make a lot of sense, but it was one of the things Michele loved best about her. They both loved words. But her Mother, who ran a small advertising agency and could write a perfect sentence, always talked in twists and turns.

"Do you mean *Bath* is a place?" asked Michele.

"I do — and you and Michael are going to spend about six weeks there this summer with John. I have an out of town assignment that will take me that long, but I'll be down on weekends."

"Oh, Mother," Michele and Michael groaned together. "No!"

"We want to spend the summer with our friends at the pool," Michele said.

"Yeah, and we have tickets to the summer movies," added Michael.

"Please don't do this to us," Michele begged. "We'll just die."

"You'll live," she assured them. "Bath's a pretty coastal town on the Pamlico Sound. John is staying in a nice motel on Bath Creek. He's doing some historical research, so he can give you a real basement-to-attic tour of the historic homes there."

"Ugh," pouted Michael. "Is there a pool?" he asked, sliding off of the bench and onto the floor.

Mother shook her head. "Nope, no pool."

"A movie theater or skating rink?" Michele questioned, afraid she already knew the answer.

Mother's hair swished negatively again. "No, sorry," she said.

"Phooey," Michael mumbled from under the table.

Michele knew he was really upset. She was too, but hated to show it. Her Mother had to travel a good bit for her job, and Michele knew it was difficult for her to get care for them since her Mother and Father were divorced. Mom was very particular about who she left them with, and Michele figured she must have gone to a lot of trouble to arrange for them to stay with John in Bath.

John was nice, but she sure wanted to stay home this summer. Why did it seem like things always turned out differently than you planned them? It was just like her typing. She would aim for an *a* but strike the *z*.

"Well, Bath does have one redeeming factor, if you want to call it that," Mother said mysteriously. "Blackbeard lived there."

Michael popped up from under the table and screwed his nose and eyes together in disbelief.

"*The* Blackbeard?" he asked.

"No Michael, the other Blackbeard," Michele teased.

"Blackbeard, the fiercest pirate of them all," Mother said.

Michele sighed, revealing the dismay she'd been trying to

conceal. "Well, I guess we *could* spend the summer looking for treasure."

"Be sure and check Teach's Hole," Mother advised.

"I wish they would put *my* teacher in a hole," said Michael.

"*Teach's* Hole," repeated Mother. "That's where Blackbeard fought his last skull-and-crossbones battle. He lost it," she said in a deep, late show-spooky-movie voice. "And he lost his head."

"Is *that* the head you said was missing?" cried Michele. She blushed, realizing she'd just given away that she'd been eavesdropping.

"Big ears!" Mother said. "I guess you could say that Blackbeard the Pirate's head *is* missing — missing from his body. But the head they're searching so frantically for in Bath belongs to the living Blackbeard."

She sighed and said seriously, as though again reconsidering letting them go to Bath. "They must find it soon. It may be life or death for the play."

"What living Blackbeard? What head? What play?" Michele begged.

"They have an outdoor drama in Bath every summer," Mother explained. "The play is about Blackbeard and pirates and Bath. They stage it in an outdoor theater by the water."

"You mean you just sit right outside with no roof?" asked Michael.

"The sky is your roof," Michele said, then added quickly, "But what about the head?"

"In the play, just as it happened in real life, Blackbeard is killed at Teach's Hole off Ocracoke Island. They chop off his head," Mother said. "At the climax of the drama, they have a big pirate battle and end the play by holding up Blackbeard's gruesome-looking head. It's supposed to be very realistic and dramatic. But now the head is missing."

"Why don't they just make another one?" Michele asked.

"That takes time and money," Mother said. "The play is very expensive to produce and they don't try to make any money — just cover expenses. Opening night is in a couple of weeks. They need to recover the head, and find out who would risk the play's success like that — and why."

To Michele, summer in Bath was beginning to sound more mysterious, and therefore, more fun every minute.

"Tell us more about Bath," Michele said.

"Bath is North Carolina's oldest town, incorporated in 1705," Mother explained. "They have restored several historic homes. The play and the homes bring needed income to the community. A lot of mysterious shenanigans won't help the tourist business any. And, no tourist — no play!"

Suddenly, Michael grabbed his neck as though he were trying to pluck it from his shoulders. "Yiiii, ye got me head," he moaned.

Mother laughed. "If somebody chopped off your head today, they'd get squirted with soapsuds instead of blood," she said, taking the kitchen towel and rubbing his hair.

"Yiiii, it was me own Mother," Michael squealed, holding his neck and letting his head flop left and right under the towel.

"But who would steal the head and jeopardize the play?" pondered Michele.

Mother laughed. "A play's the ultimate treasure, hey? I don't know who would steal a prop head," she said, looking worried. "But John promised he would keep you two, as well as Jo Dee and Brian, from playing detective until it's found and the play can begin."

"Who's Jo Dee?" Michael asked excitedly. He poked his head out from under the towel. "Who's Brian? Does he have a head?"

"John's two children will be staying with him this summer," Mother explained.

"Oh brother," groaned Michele. "I guess I'll have to babysit." That's what summer had meant for the last couple of years since Mother started working. Michele had to watch Michael several mornings or afternoons each week, and she liked for them to stay close to home. Of course it meant extra spending money, and Michele had to admit it was hard to find ways to earn money when you're only twelve.

"Brian's thirteen, so I doubt he'd appreciate you as a babysitter," Mother said.

"Super!" said Michael. "Is Jo Dee a boy too?"

"Sorry, Jo Dee is a ten-year-old girl," Mother said.

"Girls! They're taking over the world!" Michael complained. "They're everywhere, and they're all older than me. It isn't fair!"

Michele laughed. She guessed it was hard sometimes to be the youngest and the only boy in the family, especially now with Dad not around. She knew Michael missed him. Maybe that's why Mom had arranged for them to stay with John for awhile, she thought.

Mother swatted Michael's hair with the towel once more and stood up. "I'd better fix you pirates some grog and hardtack for lunch," she said and went into the kitchen.

"We'll find the head when we're in Bath," Michele whispered to Michael, hoping Mother wasn't eavesdropping.

"Phooey with Blackbeard's head," said Michael, "let's find his treasure!" He watched as Michele pecked out on the computer keyboard:

"Who has the head? Why? What will they do next?"

The phone rang and Mother answered it and came around the corner with a strange look on her face.

She thrust the receiver toward Michele as though she were eager to get rid of it. "It's for you," she said. "It's Blackbeard."

2 PHONE CALL FROM A PIRATE

Michele stared at Mother in disbelief. Then she took the receiver carefully. She'd never talked to a pirate before. "Hello?" she said, her voice quivering in suspense.

"Good morning, Miss Hunt," said a man's voice, deep and rich sounding like their minister had. "My name is Jack Denning. I'm an actor and will play the part of Ned Teach — Blackbeard — in the outdoor drama in Bath this summer."

An actor! Michele thought he sounded handsome and friendly to be a pirate. But of course, that was only in the play, she reminded herself.

"I'm at the Harbor Motel," he continued. "John was telling me about you and your planned visit to Bath, and of your interest in the theater."

"Oh yes, Mr. Blackbeard — I mean, Mr. Denning, I love the theater," she said.

"Well, I was wondering if you'd be interested in helping us out during this summer's performance?" he asked casually.

"Help?" Michele repeated in awe.

"Yes. We're lining up students your age to help with tickets, concessions, props — maybe even be an extra in one of the scenes."

Michele couldn't believe he was offering her a chance to be in, around, and maybe even on the stage.

9

"Of course you might have to help clean up afterwards too," he added.

Clean up! Didn't he know that to be near the theater she would sweep the entire stage with one hand and the broom behind her back?

"And," he added, "the pay's not much."

Pay! They were going to let her do all this and pay her too, Michele marveled. Why, she would offer them her lifetime allowance for an opportunity like this.

Her cheeks flushed as she realized the actor had quit talking and was waiting for her to speak.

"You bet!" she wanted to shout into the telephone. She smiled mysteriously at Mother and Michael who were staring at her, puzzled. "I'll have to ask my Mother," she said, trying to sound like that was just a simple technicality.

"Well, be sure and tell her there's a lot of adult supervision, especially since my head has disappeared," he said with a deep laugh.

He sure did sound like a pirate, Michele thought.

"Please let me or Tom Tankard, the play manager, know your decision just as soon as you get to Bath," he said.

"I will," Michele assured him. "Thank you! Goodbye."

Michele sat on the bench holding the receiver tightly in her hand, not moving.

"Was that *really* Blackbeard?" Michael asked, his hands tucked under his chin in fright. "Why didn't you let me talk to him?"

"What did he want?" Mother asked.

"He wanted me to work at the play this summer," Michele

said. She looked pleadingly at her Mother. "He said there would be a lot of adult supervision. And John will be there. Can I please?" she begged.

Mother sat back down across the breakfast table from Michele and gave her that same loving once over. She was quiet. Then slowly and sadly she shook her head. "No dear, I'm afraid not, at least not until they solve the reason for any thievery around the theater."

"Mother!" Michele said, "You can't mean it — it's my chance of a lifetime. Oh, please!"

"I know it's an unusual opportunity," agreed Mother. "But I'm not going to be there to keep an eye on you, you know. And I'll worry if you're roaming around some dark theater at midnight while somebody's up to meanness. John has a lot of research to do and I can't bother him by having him go around the theater until this missing head mystery is solved."

"Oh please, Mother," Michele repeated, but this time half-heartedly. "Will you at least think about it?" she begged.

"Of course, dear," Mother promised, reaching over the computer and patting Michele's hand. "If John says they've found the thief by the time we get to Bath, I'll reconsider, but otherwise . . ."

"Can I be in the play too?" Michael asked. "Can I be a pirate?"

"Some pirate you'd make," Michele said. "Blackbubble the Pest."

Mother frowned. "You'd make a very good pirate," she said. "Get dry and let's see how much you've outgrown last summer's clothes. John, Jo Dee, and Brian are looking for you in Bath next week," she added, hustling Michael upstairs.

Michele slammed the computer shut. How could Mother make her miss a chance like this, she wondered. Her dream was a career in the theater. She used to think she wanted to be a playwright. But when she had shop class in school last year, she decided she wanted to design and build sets. After taking sewing and home economics, she thought she'd rather be a costumer.

Then, after her first trip to the dinner theater in Raleigh, she felt certain she should be an actress.

Ever since, she had watched for an opportunity to try out even one theatrical job. But when they had the community children's theater last summer, she had a broken leg and couldn't participate.

Her school's new drama club was limited to 25 members. Participants for next year would be selected on "demonstrated interest and ability," as the school called it. It was like she had heard teenagers say about job hunting. You have to have experience to get one, but you can't get experience if no one will give you a job in the first place.

Michele sighed. Sometimes she was afraid she would turn out like Aunt Mae who started to go to college to be a science teacher, but dropped out, got married and had little Sammy. The last time Michele saw her, she was washing Sammy's sister's diapers and watching those silly soap operas on tv. The only experiments she ever got to make were in the kitchen on new dinner recipes. Michele believed that if Aunt Mae had just gotten her degree first she could still have had Sammy and Sissy and been able to teach, too.

If she could just get in the drama club next year, she could try out a lot of different theater jobs and decide what she wanted to concentrate on when she went to the East Carolina University Drama School in Greenville.

As she put away her homework, Michele realized that the best chance to be in the play was for her to solve the mystery of the missing head — and solve it *fast!*

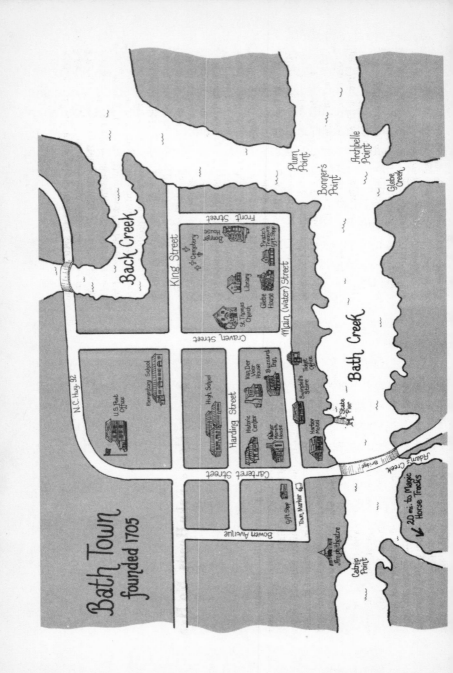

3 REAL HEADS, FAKE HEADS, NO HEADS

Bright and early on June 10th, Michael and Michele stuffed their suitcases with shorts, sneakers and swimsuits, and headed for Bath.

Not long after they left the rolling hills of Raleigh, they hit the flatter, Coastal Plain section of the state. The sky was electric blue, like looking into the deep end of a swimming pool, and the trees were as green as lime popsicles.

This was tobacco country and the little sucker plants had been set out in neat rows. Michele thought smoking was a stupid habit. She couldn't understand why people enjoyed sucking hot smoke down into their throats when you heard so much about how bad it was for your lungs. But there was not a much prettier growing crop than tobacco, especially when it topped out in the fall with its little white corsage of blossoms budding above the fat, green leaves.

Once when Mother was writing an article on the tobacco industry, Michele had gone with her to a tobacco auction in Rocky Mount. Even though she could hardly stand the smell in the hot warehouse, it was exciting to watch the parade of buyers led by the auctioneer through the mounds of brown tobacco as he gave his speedy mumble-jumble sales pitch.

Michele fiddled with her camera as they drove along. She saw a lot of sights that would make good pictures. Mother was

15

very quiet and Michele wondered if she was still having second thoughts about bringing them to Bath.

Michael was bugging them both by keeping a running tally of how many telephone poles, cows, and horses they passed. He also kept asking when they would stop for hamburgers and french fries, although it was only nine o'clock in the morning.

When they reached the Bath Creek Bridge, Michele begged Mother to stop and let her take a picture. The tiny town stretched out on the banks of the bay like it was posing for a postcard. Little buildings of yellow, white, and blue nestled in the green pines along the shoreline. A weathered gray pier lined with colorful bobbing sailboats jutted out into the glistening blue water.

The car bumped off the edge of the road onto the gravel shoulder. Michael hopped out as soon as they stopped and hung over the concrete rail of the bridge. "Can we swim now?" he asked excitedly.

"Get down!" Mother warned.

"I can't wait to see the rest of the town," Michele said.

"This is just about it," Mother said with a chuckle. "Except for the historic district on beyond, you can see most of Bath from here. There are only a few hundred people and the town is only one mile long and a half dozen blocks wide."

"Where's the theater?" Michele asked.

Mother pointed past the left side of the bridge to the opposite shore. "Over there where you see the mast of a boat sticking up out of the trees."

"Hey look," Michael called, motioning across the bay. At the end of the pier stood two dark-headed children waving their arms.

"Brian and Jo Dee look eager to meet you," Mother said.

Michele waved back. She got along well with boys. She just hoped Brian wouldn't rub in being a year older than her and a teenager.

They drove slowly over the bridge and up to the motel. Jo Dee was jumping up and down on the porch and waving something at them.

When they got out of the car, Jo Dee's eyes, magnified into big, brown pools behind her glasses, looked Michael over critically. Then she grinned and handed him a small card. "It's a ticket to the opening night of the outdoor drama," she said.

Brian scowled at Michele, "*If* there's an opening night," he muttered.

Michael screwed his eyes and nose together as he took the ticket. "Hey," he said, pointing to the skull and crossbones printed on the card, "this ticket's poison."

"Yeah," said Brian, "don't eat it."

Everyone laughed except Michael who looked like he could chew up the ticket and spit it out, and Michele, who didn't really like the way Brian teased her brother.

Brian thrust a ticket at Michele. Well, she thought, even if she couldn't be in the play yet, she guessed she might as well watch it. Maybe she could get some clues to solve the mystery. Of course, it was going to be difficult to get any help finding the missing head from a grumpy boy like this.

Absent-mindedly, she turned the ticket over in her hand. On the back someone had sketched a hairy head. Scrawled underneath was: *"Where do you think it is?"*

Michele looked up at Brian in surprise and smiled. "I don't know," she whispered. *"Yet!"*

Suddenly from behind them, someone bellowed, "Yo ho ho!"

The door to one of the downstairs motel rooms opened. A tall, stocky, handsome man came out, smiling broadly, his arms outstretched as though to encompass them all. "Welcome to Bath!" he shouted.

Michele wasn't sure she liked the way he hugged and kissed her Mother, but she could tell it was all right with her.

"Hello John," Mother said, hugging him back. "I'm delivering the rest of your crew."

"Delighted to have them aboard," John said. "We'll take the grand tour of Bath in a minute."

"It'll only take a minute too," said Brian, waving his tanned arm toward the historic area.

"You show Michael and Michele their rooms," John said to Brian. "And hang on tight to those tickets so we can go to the play," he added.

As they started up the stairs to their room, Michele overheard John say to Mother, *"If* they have the play. They still haven't found the missing head."

Michele slowed her steps and stayed behind the others, eavesdropping again in spite of herself.

"Oh John," Mother said, "I don't like the sound of this. Can you keep the kids out of mischief and get all your work done too?"

"Don't worry," John assured her, "I'll keep them occupied.

Whoever's 'a-pyrating' will be caught soon, I'm sure. Maybe Michele can still be in the play before the end of the season."

"Well, I don't want my kids anywhere around the theater until this mystery is all cleared up," Mother insisted.

Oh, brother, Michele thought. She sure hoped John had enough work to do to keep from watching them closely.

The others had already disappeared up the steep, narrow staircase when Michele closed the door behind her and followed them.

The motel really looked like a house from the front. It was divided into four sections. Two downstairs rooms were like apartments with a bed, table and chairs and kitchen area. Upstairs, there was a big room with a bath on each side of the hall that Mother had rented for her children.

"This is really neat," Michele said as she caught up with the others. Then she spotted the best thing of all — the view of Bath Creek stretching out into Bath Bay, the Pamlico River, and on beyond sight, the Pamlico Sound and the Graveyard of the Atlantic where so many ships had been wrecked on the dangerous sandbars in the shallow waters.

"That's Bonner's Point," explained Brian, pointing to the nearest piece of land sticking out in the water.

"It looks like a super place for a picnic," Michele noted. It was not like a beach, but grassy with trees and water around three sides.

"See that place with sand on it?" Brian asked, pointing on beyond Bonner's Point. "That's Plum Point, where Ned Teach lived when he was in Bath," Brian said.

"Blackbeard?" asked Michael.

"Blackbeard!" said Jo Dee.

"What did Ned Teach do while he was in Bath?" Michele asked. She could see Brian liked to show off his knowledge of pirates, but she was too curious to care. Besides, the sooner she got started on this mystery, the better.

"He married some local girl," he said in disgust. "She wasn't much older than you."

"He was supposed to have had about fourteen wives," Jo Dee said.

"Yuck!" said Michael, "That would be as bad as having fourteen mothers or fourteen teachers."

Brian laughed, and Michele was relieved to see he wasn't always so grim. Maybe he was just as unhappy as she had been at first about spending the summer away from home and friends. Of course, that was before she had a chance to be in a play.

Brian looked back out the window. "Some people say Blackbeard built a tunnel from Plum Point under the bay to Archbell Point on the other side. Governor Eden lived there and he kind of ignored Blackbeard's pirating."

"And sharing some of his booty was Blackbeard's way of paying him off?" Michele asked.

Brian turned and nodded in admiration. He seemed impressed that she would figure that out.

"Tell us what Blackbeard's head looks like," Michael begged.

They all plopped on the soft, squashy bed as Brian described the famous orb.

"It has blackety-black stiff hair all over and a long, wiry, tangled beard," he explained. "The eyes are black and have an evil look. And the face has smoke marks from where he would tuck burning candles in his beard to look scary."

"But it really isn't Blackbeard's head that's missing," Brian added. "The actor playing Blackbeard in the play had a scary costume head."

"At the end of the play when Blackbeard gets his head cut off, another pirate is supposed to hold up the costume head like it is the real one and the audience goes *Ghhhaaa!*" Jo Dee said.

"Which head?" asked Michael.

"Blackbeard's!" they all shouted at him, rolling on the bed and laughing at how confusing it was.

Michele sat up. "How many heads are there?"

"None right now," Brian said. "That's the problem. The fake head was specially-made by a costumer in Washington to look real. You can't just go to the store and pick up a large head of Blackbeard the Pirate, you know. They've rush-ordered another one, but it's going to take some time. It won't be ready for the opening."

"What will they do when the part of the play comes where they need the head?" Michele asked.

"In rehearsal, the pirate just points his cutlass up at the bowsprit of the ship and everyone looks up. I guess you're supposed to use your imagination. But it sure takes away from the ending if you've ever seen the real head," Brian told her.

"You said it was fake," Michael reminded him.

They laughed. It really was confusing.

"Would you like to volunteer your head for the play?" Brian asked in a spooky voice, reaching his outstretched fingers towards Michael's neck.

Michael jumped off the bed.

"Well, imagination is good when you're reading," Michele said, "but I can see where they need the real head for the play — and I think I can help them."

"How?" asked Brian, doubtfully.

"Is there a way I can see what Blackbeard's head looked like?" Michele asked.

"There's a gift shop near the entrance to the theater," Jo Dee said. "A local artist did a big picture of Blackbeard to go over the door."

Michele scrambled off the bed. "Let's go!" she said.

Even the short walk to the Pirate's Treasure gift shop left them breathless. It was a hot summer day, the kind where the heavy, humid air feels like it's holding onto you.

When they reached the shop, they fell down on the cool grass and stared up at the sign with Blackbeard's face painted on it in black and red and yellow.

"He would surely be a frightening sight to see coming toward you," Michele agreed.

"Especially with bandoliers full of pistols and a cutlass in his hand," said Brian.

"And candles burning in his beard," added Jo Dee.

"They say some pirate ships surrendered just at the sight of him," Brian said.

"I would if I saw him," Jo Dee agreed.

"I *did* see him," said Michael, softly.

"When?" challenged Brian. "Where?"

"Over there," Michael answered, and Michele knew from his quiet, matter-of-fact tone that he was *not* kidding!

4 SPOOKY MAN, STRANGE SACK

They all turned and looked to where Michael was pointing.

Trudging down Water Street toward them was a tall, gangly, stoop-shouldered man. He looked young, Michele thought, but sad and very tired. His head and chin were covered with bushy, black hair. He wore knee-high, muddy boots and clutched a brown canvas sack that hung almost to the ground. The rounded bottom of the bag strained from whatever was inside of it.

The strange young man kept his head and eyes lowered as he tramped closer. They all lay perfectly still in the grass, as though they were frozen in a game of "statues" until someone tagged them.

"He's coming at us!" Jo Dee whispered.

"Wonder what's in that sack?" muttered Brian.

As the man reached the opposite street corner his black eyes darted up once. Then he turned sharply on the heel of a mud-caked boot and he and the bobbing brown sack disappeared into the trees.

A voice behind them caused them to jump. "Ain't you kids shoppin' today?"

"Yes sir," Michele assured the man, knowing it was not very polite to camp out on his store step and not at least window-shop. He reminded her of one of those neat porcelain carvings of sailors that looked so lifelike. His face had been fried by the sun and wind and his eyes were the gray color of a cold sea. He was small but his muscles were tight beneath his tee shirt.

"Who's the guy with the beard, Ben?" Brian asked.

"Don't know son," Ben said. "He's been around since school's out, and I see him make that trip every day this time. Always looks plum beat."

"Does he always have that sack with him?" asked Michele.

"Sure does. Don't know what he's got in it, but he sure holds onto it for dear life," said Ben, as he turned and went back inside.

Michele and Brian followed. She sure didn't want Ben to suspect their real reason for shopping, even if no one knew that yet except for her.

Michael and Jo Dee were already exploring the cramped, crowded shop. "Yo ho ho!" Michael squealed, waving a plastic pirate flag and pulling a paper pirate hat down over his eyes.

Michele began weaving her way through the gift shop. The plastic and pine trinkets looked more like junk than treasure to her. But she knew exactly the things she needed, if she could just find them.

"You kids going to the play opening?" Ben asked. "If anything else happens to the play this summer I guess we won't have one next year." Ben shook his head and the wrinkles in his brow seemed to triple. "Ha! If we ever get to have one this year. I really count on those tourists buying lil' souvenirs. If the outdoor drama closes, I may have to close too."

"I guess a lot of people count on the play continuing," Michele said as she fished through a barrel of tangled yarn.

"Sure do," Ben said. "It really helps the local economy through ticket sales and giving people jobs. The amphitheater is a real asset to the town. And the play's a super way for those East Carolina University drama students to get some experience. Of course," he added, "some people would be just as happy if the play did fold."

"You're kidding!" said Michele, in surprise.

"You have to remember," said Ben, "that this has been a quiet, little town for a long time. The play means traffic and a lot of strangers roaming around all over the place. I guess when you live around historic things for a while you just take them for granted."

"If they lived in a big city like I do and see developers tear down neat old places to make parking lots, they wouldn't," Michele said. "Do you think that whoever stole the head wants to see the outdoor drama fail?" she asked.

"You bet!" said Ben. "And I think the missing head is just the beginning unless the scoundrel is caught."

Caught soon, Michele thought, as she wandered down the last aisle. Finally she brought an odd assortment of items and dumped them on the counter.

Ben looked surprised at her purchases. "Things aren't always what they seem," he said mysteriously.

"What does that mean?" Michele asked. "Do you know something, Ben?"

"I just know Bath's a small town. Some people have been opposed to the development of the historic district. Some folks just don't think progress is all it's cracked up to be. Of course, you can't necessarily blame them. Front Street used to be our Main Street. The dry goods, drug store, barber shop, meat market, blacksmith, and other stores were always bustling. The Palmer-Marsh house was a hotel. There was a lumber mill, two theaters, and a lodge hall. A showboat even stopped here."

"A showboat?" questioned Michele.

"Yep," said Ben. "A regular floating theater. It would dock at the pier, and the townspeople would gather on the shore to see the play staged on the boat's bow."

"Oh, Ben!" Michele swooned, "Does it still stop here ?"

Ben shook his head. "When the new bridge was built over Bath Creek it became the main highway and our business district was bypassed. The new road was built to keep traffic off Main Street and shorten the distance through Bath. And it did just that, much to the shopowners' dismay. So it *was* progress, but it sure hurt some of us, and the problems it caused has carried over into citizen's attitudes today. We don't even have a showboat anymore," Ben added sadly.

Discouraged, Michele left the shop with her secret bag of treasures. The others had sprawled out on the grass again, and were drinking icy orange drinks out of cold, sweating bottles.

"You're not yo-ho-hoed out, are you?" Michele teased her brother.

"No-ho-ho!" Michael said, hopping up and striking a silly swashbuckler pose in his new pirate hat purchase.

"You look absolutely ferocious," Brian said and laughed.

"You really do," Michele assured her brother. "Maybe later I can make a black patch for one eye."

"Yo ho ho — thanks!" Michael shouted. "C'mon, Jo Dee, let's turn that deck behind the motel into a pirate ship. I'll be Blackbeard. You can be my first mate."

"Not me," Jo Dee said stubbornly. "I'll be Anne Bonny. Women were pirates too, you know, and they could be just as mean as the men."

"Ferocious!" Michele said, noting that it was Brian's turn to frown when she teased his sister.

The two pretend pirates started across the street still arguing over who was the most bloodthirsty buccaneer.

Brian turned to Michele. "What's in the bag?" he asked suspiciously. "Your solution to the mystery?"

"Let's go over to the amphitheater and I'll show you," Michele said. "I think we're going to find the missing head," she added smugly, "and solve this silly mystery fast."

She turned on her heel and Brian followed impatiently. Ben stuck his head out of the gift shop door and hollered. "Don't lose your own head over this missing head mystery, Miss Michele!"

Michele laughed, but felt her throat tighten as though some invisible hand had squeezed her neck in a warning.

The amphitheater was at Catnip Point on Bath Creek. The parking area was really an old orchard. Even on such a hot day as this, it was cool beneath the sprawling branches.

The outdoor stage was right on the water's edge. It looked like a fort with its high picket fence around the back and sides. The empty weatherboard stage seemed abandoned in the bright sunlight.

Michele headed toward a big tree near the corner of the theater where the breeze from the bay would cool them. She fell to her knees and dumped the things she had just bought on the grass.

"What's all this garbage?" Brian asked, picking through the strange assortment: a box of modeling clay; black yarn; a bottle of glue; a pack of colored marking pens; two big cat's eye marbles; and a box of candles.

"This is the *found* head of Blackbeard," Michele said proudly.

"Oh, yeah?" said Brian. Then his eyes sparkled in understanding. "Y-e-a-h — and the play goes on!"

"And the play goes on with me in it," Michele said, "See, if we mold this clay into a face, stick on marble eyes, use black yarn for the hair and beard, and color in features like the cheekbones with the markers, do you think it will look like the head that disappeared?"

"Well . . ." Brian hesitated, "Not exactly, but close enough, especially from the audience. But the other head had a white cloth around the neck like it was the top of Blackbeard's shirt. I'll bet we could find some fabric backstage . . . c'mon!"

"How can we get in?" Michele asked, as she followed Brian through the woods along the steep bank of Bath Creek.

"The front of the stage looks like a pirate ship, but the very back of the stage is open," Brian said, pointing to the masts jutting from behind the stage up through the pines.

Michele was amazed at the clever construction of the ship which had openings in the side and floor to allow the actors to get on board without being seen by the audience. It gave her butterflies in her stomach just to climb up through it.

When she reached the shipdeck-stage, she stood still and stared out into the hot sunlight at the rows of empty seats. If only she could have a chance to be on stage just once. She could almost hear the phantom applause of the invisible spectators.

"Michele!" Brian called impatiently. He had disappeared through the black curtain that covered the entrance and exit to the stage. "There's some fabric laying around back here," he called.

Reluctantly, Michele left the stage and found Brian in a dark shadowy corner kneeling over a wrinkled roll of cloth. "Won't do," she said. "Whoever heard of a pirate in a flowered shirt? Maybe there's some white cloth in here," she added, heading toward a door.

"Maybe," Brian said, "but that's the prop room and it's locked, so we can't go in there."

"I can't *be* in the play . . . I can't even *see* the play unless we find that head," Michele said, kicking the plank door angrily.

She and Brian gasped as the supposedly locked door slowly creaked open. Shoulder-to-shoulder they slipped inside the room and stood very still. It was dark, but their eyes soon adjusted to the small amount of light that seeped through the cracks between the boards. The narrow room was crowded with a hodgepodge of furniture. Tables, chairs, and lanterns were stacked against the walls. Tin ale tankards were scattered all around.

"Look," said Brian, motioning to an old trunk in the corner of the room. "That's where they kept the head."

Still side by side they moved slowly towards the trunk. "It isn't locked," Michele said, pointing to the dangling latch.

"Not since the head was swiped," Brian said. "No sense locking an empty trunk."

Michele thought Brian said the word "empty" with doubt. Her hand trembled as she reached for the loose clasp and pulled the domed lid open.

They both released the breaths that had bottled-up inside them.

"It *is* empty," Michele said, relieved, yet disappointed. "It doesn't look as large open as it does closed," she noted.

Brian bent down to take a good look inside the trunk. "When we get our new head made we can slip it in here before they discover the door . . ."

Suddenly, just as he said the word "door," the door behind them slammed shut.

5 THE THIEF STRIKES AGAIN

The walls shook as though the entire room would collapse. Michele dropped the trunk lid and spun around to see the door creaking back open again. "Thank goodness, we're not locked in," she said.

There was a muffled scurry of footsteps. They grabbed one of the pirate's swords piled in the corner, and ran onto the stage.

"Over there!" Brian shouted, stabbing his sword in the air toward the bow of the pirate ship.

Michele looked in time to see a dark-headed man in a pirate hat disappear overboard. She darted after him, but skidded and fell.

Brian grabbed her by the arm. "Let's go," he urged.

"Wait! Look!" Michele demanded, pulling away. She pointed to the spot where she had first slid. "Muddy bootprints," she said.

"I'd say someone is trying to scare us away from looking for the head," Brian said.

"We should tell John," said Michele.

Brian picked the swords up and put them back in the prop room and closed the door. "Then we'll have to explain what we were doing here," he reminded her.

They crossed the stage and as Michele climbed the steps

to the upper deck, she glanced over her shoulder at the rows of empty seats. It seemed less likely than ever that she would get in the play. But she could imagine the audience snuggled together against the cool night air. Their faces would be uplifted toward the stage, their eyes wide with anticipation of the unfolding events of the play. She, of course, would be on center stage, putting her all into her performance, then bowing modestly at the thunderous applause that would follow.

She turned and jumped off the back side of the ship and climbed the hillside to the tree where they had left the makings for a new head. When she reached the spot, she stopped short and put her hands on her hips in disgust.

Some of the things had been scattered in the dirt. The yarn was chopped in pieces like spaghetti. The crayons were broken in half. And the clay had been opened and lay melting in the hot sun like a big blob of pink chewing gum.

Brian motioned down to the bay and Michele saw the marking pens bobbing in the water like colorful sailboats. "Someone doesn't want there to be a head, old or new," he said. "Someone with black hair and muddy boots."

Angrily, Michele stooped down and scooped up a handful of dusty yarn and tossed it into the bay.

"We didn't see his face," she reminded him. "So we don't know if it was the bearded man with the sack or not."

They walked slowly back to the motel in silence. Mother was putting her camera gear into the car. It seemed to Michele that every time her Mother got near someone who was also a writer or photographer they had to drag out all the projects they were working on and talk about them forever.

But she guessed that's the way it is when you're lucky enough to work in something you love. She could just imagine being part of a cast and sitting around all hot and sweaty after a performance, talking about how well everything had gone, and what a good audience it was, and laughing over someone losing their false eyelash right in the middle of the third act.

"You kids be good, now, you hear," Mother said, hugging each of them tightly, even Jo Dee and Brian. "And *don't* try and solve this mystery — and I mean it!" she warned, looking Michele straight in the eye.

Michele and Brian exchanged guilty glances.

"I'll keep a sharp lookout on this crew," John assured her.

"*You* even sound like a pirate," Mother teased.

"*I'm* the pirate," Michael said, swishing his cardboard sword through the air. "I'll protect us all."

"You just keep that thing out of your eye and everyone else's," Mother begged. "And somewhere between all the playing and swimming, take time out to see the historic sites."

"They're just old houses," Brian said.

John and Mother shook their heads in exasperation. "*Historic* old houses, Brian," John corrected him.

Mother hugged and kissed John, and with one last everyone-behave-yourself look, she drove across the Bath Creek bridge and out of sight.

Michael and Jo Dee, still whooping "Yo-ho-ho!," headed for their back porch pirate ship.

John nodded at Michele and Brian, "You two come inside a minute," he said seriously.

Michele felt worried. Maybe someone had told him that they were at the amphitheater. If they got grounded, they'd never be able to solve the mystery before the play opened.

John motioned for them to sit down at the table by the window. He stared out at the calm blue bay as he talked.

"Something's happened," he said. "I didn't want your mother to know. She'd only worry, and she's got a lot of work to do this summer." He turned and looked at them. "I had a call from the ticket office. Now someone has taken all the theater keys."

"When?" Brian asked.

"Last night," said John. "Tank had set them on the concession stand while he moved some fallen limbs from the parking area. The keys just disappeared."

Michele and Brian stared at each other knowingly. So that's why the prop room was open, Michele thought.

"It could have been . . ." Brian began, and Michele kicked his shin sharply beneath the table.

Brian grimaced and Michele bit her lip back at him in apology, but she'd had to shush him.

"What do you mean?" John asked. Then not waiting for an answer, he banged his fist on the table, startling them both. "If this thievery keeps up, I doubt they'll open the play at all."

Michele looked glumly down at the table. She was really confused about the who, what, when, where and why of this mystery. But one thing seemed clear — almost anything could happen. She remembered what Ben had said to her.

"Nothing's like it seems," she muttered.

"What?" asked John.

Now it was Brian's turn to kick Michele back under the table. Michele muffled an "*Ouch!*" Boy he kicked hard, she thought, and he didn't even look sorry.

She pretended she hadn't heard John, and he went back to staring out the window.

Brian looked questioningly at Michele. She knew he was wondering whether or not to tell his Dad about the man with the beard and sack . . . the man with the muddy boots who might have been the one to scare them at the theater. She tried to think of a way to communicate, "*Don't do it.*" Putting her hands on the table, she made a circle with her thumb and finger, then covered it with the crossed fore and middle finger of her other hand.

At first, Brian looked puzzled, but then he smiled and nodded understandingly at the skull and crossbones sign. It was a signal they would use a lot in the next eventful few weeks.

6 A Clue Comes Ashore

The next morning Michele awoke with a start in the little room above Bath Creek. All night she had tossed and turned, dreaming of all sorts of heads, in all kinds of places, from the bowsprits of ships to washing up on the shore right outside her door.

Now in the morning light only one had come to mind — Blackbeard's. But she could not imagine where it could be. They simply didn't have any clues to work with.

Her thoughts were interrupted by the thump-thutter-thump of something clambering up the hall steps.

Michael burst into her room. "Come see what Fuzzbucket found! Hurry!" he squealed.

"What?" Michele mumbled irritably, hoisting herself up on one elbow and rubbing her eyes. "What's a bucket of fuzz?"

"Fuzzbucket is the duck who lives at the motel," Michael explained. "Come see what he found. You won't believe it! Hurry!"

"*Fuzzbucket,*" Michele muttered, untangling her feet from the sheets. She shooed Michael out and then slipped on a pair of shorts and a tee shirt and followed him down the steps.

Yawning and stretching, Jo Dee and Brian stumbled out onto the deck to see what the commotion was all about.

They tiptoed sleepily through the dewy grass to the water's

edge. Then suddenly, they were as wide awake as Michael.

"See!" Michael said, falling on his knees and stretching out over the edge of the water sloshing against the bank.

Fuzzbucket circled a small corked bottle inching its way toward the shore. He quacked noisily as though he were claiming the discovery. With each bob of a wave, the brown glass glittered in the morning, winking at them teasingly.

Trying to avoid the snapping mousetrap mouth of the duck, Michele reached for the bottle.

Michael and Jo Dee jumped from one foot to another. Brian stood perfectly still watching every bounce of the bottle as though it would disappear if he took his eyes off it.

A wave slapped the slick bottle close to Michele's outstretched hand. She grabbed it.

"Got it!" Michael and Jo Dee squealed together.

"Sssh," Brian warned. "We don't want to wake John up."

Michele set the dripping bottle on the ground and they all huddled around it. Even Fuzzbucket hushed and got still.

The bottle was stoppered with a chipped, bleached cork. Michele turned it over in her hand trying to see or hear what they all hoped would be inside. She felt each of their imaginations running wild as to where the bottle had come from and what message, if any, it contained. Had it accidentally washed ashore at the Harbor Motel – or, as she suspected, had it been sent almost "special delivery"? And, above all, did the bearded man have anything to do with the bottle coming to them?

"Cut out the dramatic pauses and open the thing," Brian said.

Michele nodded and tugged at the stopper.

Message from a pirate?

"A real pirate's bottle," Michael said.

"At least it's too little for any yucky old head to be in," said Jo Dee.

With a sputter of water, the cork popped out. They watched nervously as Michele turned the bottle upside down. Nothing! She shook the bottle gently from side to side and a tight roll of damp-edged paper peeked through the narrow neck. Grasping the roll gently, she slowly pulled it out.

"Open it!" Brian demanded.

Michele felt like she was in a play, being given cues from offstage. She unrolled the tight paper, and they each held down a corner of it. Michele read slowly, as though reading a script for the first time:

"Looking for the missing head . . .
Don't worry about the theater keys . . .
No matter what the play is dead —
Even if you find the room between
the twin chimneys."

"Wow," Michael marveled. "A real pirate note, written in blood."

"Sorry, Michael," Michele said, examining the note closely. "This is a piece of new paper . . . and I don't think pirates had red ink pens."

Michael looked so disappointed that Michele added quickly, "But it is our first real clue to the missing pirate head!"

"Where are the twin chimneys?" Michele asked Brian.

"I don't know," he answered. "In Bath, I guess."

"Great," Michele said. "But where? They're probably part of one of the historic houses."

"I haven't seen any of that stuff. That's just for the *tourists*," Brian said, teasing her.

"You're a tourist when you come to Raleigh," Michele retorted. "You make a lot of traffic jams and the government spends money so you can see the Governor's Mansion and the Natural History Museum, but that's your history too, you know."

Jo Dee interrupted their argument. "I think I know where the twin chimneys are," she said softly.

"Well, what are we sitting here for," Michele said eagerly. "Let's go find the room between them and get the head!"

Brian thought to snatch the bottle from Michael and hide it behind his back as they started back inside to get their tennis shoes. John met them at the door and insisted they eat breakfast, although they each denied being even a little bit hungry.

"Phooey," grumbled Michael as he slumped down in his chair.

John was sure a good cook, Michele admitted. She figured that was from being divorced and having to cook for himself. They gobbled yummy shrimp and cheese omelets. No one spoke for fear of giving away their newfound secret. But Jo Dee and Michael giggled between every bite of food.

"That duck's sure making a lot of racket," John complained. "Wonder what he's so geared up about this morning?"

Michele swallowed a smile along with a bite of toast as she watched the others quickly stuff something in their mouths and mumble an answer.

After breakfast, it was crowded cleaning up in the tiny kitchen area. John was even stricter than Mother about keeping picked up, Michele thought. He said he "ran a tight ship." Of course, he had the same rules for all of them, so it was fair, Michele thought.

When they finished the dishes, John's head was buried deep in the sports page of the newspaper. He just looked blankly over his coffee cup at them when they said they were going for a walk and would be back later.

When they were safely outside, Brian showed Michael and Jo Dee the skull and crossbones sign and suggested they use it to warn each other that something was up about the mystery when adults were around and they couldn't speak freely.

"That's a super idea," Michele agreed. "If John discovers we're working on solving the mystery, we'll be grounded forever!"

Jo Dee led the way up Water Street to Bonner's Point. The tiny town was quiet. Even though it was barely nine o'clock, the black asphalt road was beginning to steam with the humid coastal heat.

"How did such a little town as this get to be so important in North Carolina history?" Michele asked as they walked.

"For hundreds of years, before Bath became the state's first town, this area was inhabited by Indians," Brian said. "Early Bath leaders thought the town would grow into the commercial and political center of the colony."

"Did it?" asked Michele.

"It was for several years," Brian said. "Government officials met here. There were farms and plantations. The harbor was always crowded with ships."

"What happened?" Michele asked.

"Well, between the Indians and the pirates there was a lot of wear and tear on the town. Then Bath lost the capitalship to the city of New Bern. The post road that had brought so many new people here was re-routed. Bath had never become a great port because of shallow waters and treacherous inlets. So when the colonial period ended so did the big time for Bath."

"That's too bad," Michele observed. "How old is the town anyway?"

"Well," said Brian, "while America was celebrating her bicentennial in 1976, Bath had already celebrated it semiquincentennial in 1955."

"What's that?" asked Michael.

"It was Bath's 250th birthday."

"Wow," said Michael, "that's a lot of candles to blow out."

They laughed and then marched on, their steps slow and deliberate, as if they were trying to be as quiet as the town. Even Michael kept his pirate flag close by his side instead of waving it wildly around like he usually did.

Michele couldn't help but wonder if whoever had sent them the clue in the bottle was watching them now. She kept having the urge to look over her shoulder. Once she did, and saw there was someone following them. But no one with a black beard, just Tideriggings, a stray dog that hung around the motel and liked to bark at the sailboats.

They walked single file past Swindell's General Store, the outdoor drama ticket office, and an assortment of antique and gift shops.

Michele noticed that Jo Dee was leading them toward the opposite side of the street, increasing her pace with each step.

Suddenly Michele realized what Jo Dee was trying to sneak by. "What's that creepy place?" she asked, marveling at the rickety building covered with snaky kudzu vines. It looked like if you blew on it hard, it would collapse.

"It's the Buzzard Inn," Jo Dee answered, "and it gives me goosebumps on my goosebumps to walk by it."

"*Run* by it, you mean," taunted Brian.

"Why do they call it the Buzzard Inn?" asked Michael. "Because the buzzardy old pirates stayed there?"

"Buzzard was the owner's name," Brian said. "But pirates and other travelers did stay here. They came by horse and buggy and would bed down seven or eight in one room."

"Cozy," muttered Michele.

"Crowded!" said Michael.

"I'll bet there are snakes and bugs and all kinds of neat creepy-crawlies under that green vine stuff," Michael said with delight.

"Yuck!" squealed Jo Dee, walking even faster.

Just as the others started to laugh, their chuckles turned to shrieks as a small, green snake slithered across the doorless entrance to the tavern.

"Sillies," a voice behind them hissed suddenly. "It's just a harmless garter snake."

Startled, Michele turned to find herself face to face with the bearded man.

7 Snaky Buzzard Inn

His tired eyes gazed wearily at Michele. She dropped her head to avoid his stare and saw the fat canvas sack swinging just an inch from her knees. Her leg muscles tightened as her imagination filled the bag with bloody heads or squirming snakes — or maybe even brown bottles.

Behind her, the others stood still and quiet. Without another word, the stranger ducked his head and stomped away.

When he disappeared around the back of the inn, Michele breathed in relief. She took one look at the white-faced Jo Dee and the bug-eyed Michael and said to Brian, "Who *is* he?"

Brian shook his head and shrugged his shoulders. "Let's get out of here," he said. "All we need is for John to hear about a close call with a snake, poisonous or not."

"Yes!" agreed Jo Dee. "Let's go see the twin chimneys."

And get away from the Buzzard Inn, Michele thought, as they hurried on down the street.

The Bonner house sat on the town point which jutted out into Bath Creek.

"Whoever the Bonners were, they sure had a neat view to wake up to each day," Michele said, looking out at Plum Point.

"Joseph Bonner was a farmer," said Brian. "Much of the lumber he used to build the house came from a shipwreck off Ocracoke Island on the Outer Banks of North Carolina."

45

Jo Dee jiggled the fancy iron lock on the gate of the picket fence, and they all slipped into the front yard. The house, with its long front porch, looked cool and inviting. The uneven glass panes in the windows beside the big front door reflected the morning light in rippling waves like those in the bay.

Suddenly, Michael called around the corner of the house. "Hey you guys, you gotta come and see the twin chimneys. They're really here!"

Michele couldn't believe she'd almost forgotten why they'd come. She raced Brian around the side of the house to where Jo Dee was pointing upward to the sky.

Michele looked up. Sure enough the skinny necks of two chimneys stuck up on each side like they were anchoring the house in place against any storm that might rage into the bay.

"But there isn't a room between the chimneys," Brian said. "There are *rooms* — lots of them. How can we tell which is the one the clue meant?"

Michele counted seven windows. "What are all those rooms?" she asked.

"Well, it's been a long time since I've been in the house," Brian said, "but I think I remember a parlor and a big dining room downstairs. Upstairs, there's a master bedroom and kid's bedroom where the baseboards around the edge of the floor were finger-painted."

"Finger-painted?" repeated Michael.

"That was one of their ways of decorating," Jo Dee said.

"Gee Michael, maybe you could get a job as an historic painter," Brian teased.

"I can paint real good," Michael protested.

"You sure can," Michele agreed, frowning at Brian.

Brian ignored her and shook his head at the wall of bricks and windows scattered between the chimneys. She wished they could get in now, find the head, and have it in time for opening night.

"We could go to the Center, and see what time the next tour is," suggested Jo Dee.

"What's the Center?" asked Michael.

"She means the Historic Center," Brian explained. "They built it when Bath was made a historic site. They have a movie, maps, and guides give tours of the different historic houses if you buy a ticket."

"You mean you have to pay money to go in these old places?" marveled Michael.

"Of course," said Jo Dee. "That's how they help pay for the restoration of the houses, silly."

"Let's go," Brian said. "I know a shortcut." He turned quickly and led them through the backyard past an old stone well, the kitchen building, a gnarled scuppernong grapevine that looked as if it were as old as the house itself, the herb garden, and a small outbuilding.

"Maybe the head's in here," Michael said, giving the door a shove. Jo Dee and Brian laughed.

"Why don't you see?" said Brian in an I-dare-you voice.

"Ok," Michael said bravely, shoving the door open as the others snickered louder. He pranced inside, then turned around in the doorway and shrugged his shoulders. "There's nothing in here but three dumb holes in a long board."

Jo Dee and Brian burst into laughter. Michele joined them

in spite of herself.

Michael's tiny brown freckles were turning pink. "They're small, medium and large — kind of like for the three bears," he said, his face growing redder with a combination of confused anger and embarrassment.

Now the others were falling on the grass giggling.

"What's so funny?" Michael demanded.

"Can't you even guess what that building is for?" Brian asked.

"It's the necessary house," Jo Dee hinted.

"Necessary for what?" Michael said, coming back down the steps.

"For something very necessary!" Brian said.

Michael looked totally confused, his face puckered like a little pink prune.

Michele figured he'd had all the teasing he could take for one morning. "This was their bathroom!" she told him.

Michael's mouth fell open. "You mean outside? Out here? And they sat on . . . oh, brother!"

Still giggling, they marched on beneath the elm, walnut, and cedar trees towering over the smaller fig trees and dogwoods.

A rickety piece of picket fence guarded some ancient-looking tombstones that were almost hidden beneath the sprawling branches of a gigantic pecan tree. Brian slipped through a split section of rotted board and motioned for the others to follow.

"I'm glad it's daytime," Jo Dee mumbled.

Michele stopped to read one of the gray Bonner tombstones. She guessed this had been their home and wondered if they would be glad to know that it wasn't in

Shortcut through the graveyard

ruins but had been preserved for others to enjoy. But what would they think about a pirate head hidden somewhere in their house?

Michael hastened to catch up with the others. The Historic Center, or "the Center," as Jo Dee and Brian called it, was anything but historic. It was a small, new brick building. The cold blast of air that hit Michele in the face when she opened the door felt like blowing down into a glass of ice cubes.

"Good morning," one of the guides greeted them. "Would you like to see the movie?"

"What's the movie about?" Michele asked, not wanting to waste any more time. She was eager to return to the Bonner house and search for the room between the two chimneys.

"The movie's about Bath, of course," said Brian.

Michele figured he'd seen the movie plenty of times. For some reason that made her more interested in taking the time to see it herself. Plus, it would be good to sit down and cool off awhile.

The guide led them into a small auditorium. It was like having their own private showing, Michele thought. They settled down on the first row, and Michele thumbed through one of the brochures about the Historic Albemarle Tour that she had picked up in the lobby.

The room grew dark and the screen filled with a scene of endless rushing waves of the Atlantic Ocean and an aerial view of the Outer Banks. A deep-voiced narrator was explaining how this chain of islands was part of the Graveyard of the Atlantic – and like the rest of the east coast from Maine to

Florida, once the haunt of pirates.

Suddenly, Michele squeezed the brochure she still held in her hand. In her mind, she could see the last thing she'd been looking at before the lights went out – the Palmer-Marsh House. She grabbed Brian by the arm. "Let's go! I know where the twin chimneys are!"

"We all do," he said, pulling away. He continued staring at the screen.

"No!" Michele said emphatically. "We were wrong. It looked that way for sure, but . . . come and see!"

8 ROOMS IN A CHIMNEY

Brian shook Jo Dee and Michael's shoulders and motioned that he and Michele were leaving. Except for a brief "get lost" look, their eyes remained glued to the exciting movie about the bloody swashbuckling in Bath's history.

Slipping out a side door, Michele and Brian winced at the bright sunlight. They smiled self-consciously at the guide who looked surprised to see them leaving so soon.

"What's the big deal?" Brian demanded when they were outside the building.

But Michele was already striding away from the Center and Brian had to jog to catch up. She headed for the grounds of the Palmer-Marsh historic house next door. Parading past the headstones of the family cemetery, the smokehouse, and the stone well as though they were invisible, she marched directly to the back of the huge house.

Turning to Brian, who looked thoroughly aggravated at being ignored, she slung her hand upward and announced, "*There* are the twin chimneys!"

Brian looked up and gave a long, slow, whistle. He nodded repeatedly in admiration. "And *there* are the rooms in between," he replied.

The chimney base was almost as wide as the entire side of the house and nearly four feet thick. The mass of brick rose up the side of the house then separated into two identical chimneys. In the center of what seemed like thousands of bricks were two tiny windows, one above the other.

"Do those windows go into rooms?" Michele asked.

"I haven't been inside since sixth grade," Brian said, "so I don't remember. But I don't understand how you can have a room in a fireplace."

"Then come and see," said a pleasant voice behind them. Startled, they turned to see one of the Center guides in a long flowered gown leading the first group of tourists of the day toward the house.

"We'd really like to see what's in those . . ." Brian began.

". . . in the house," Michele interrupted. She didn't want anyone else to be as curious about the chimney rooms as they were.

"We've got a small group for this first tour. Why don't you join us?" the guide said, producing a large brass key from her apron pocket.

"Thank you, we will," Michele said.

But instead of following the guide, they let the others go on then tagged along. "This will give us an excuse to look around where we want to," Michele whispered to Brian.

They squirmed impatiently in the large entrance hall as the guide pointed out the exposed fifty foot ceiling beam which spanned the entire length of the house.

They strained to see beyond the hall, barely hearing the guide's well-rehearsed talk about the home's history — ". . . built in 1744 by Michael Coutanch, a French merchant . . . sold to Colonel Robert Palmer, leading Bath citizen . . . acquired by the Marsh family . . . lived here more than a century . . . home of one of the oldest families in North Carolina . . ."

"Gosh," Michele said, thinking of the many moves her family had made when Dad worked for a big drug company. "Imagine one family owning a house for one hundred years!"

After everyone had examined the parlor and oohed and aahed over the Queen Anne and Chippendale furniture, they finally reached the doors of the dining room and study. The rooms had matching fireplaces that were almost big enough to walk into.

"Look," Michele whispered, "There are doors beside each of the fireplaces."

Just as she said this the guide explained, "The unique double chimneys are joined by two-story pent closets which were used for storage."

"Yeah," muttered Brian, "Store *heads*."

"I hope!" Michele whispered back.

When the guide led the others upstairs, they strayed behind. Michele looked frustrated at the velvet ropes blocking the doors to the rooms. "We've got to get in those closets!" she said urgently.

Overhead she could hear the footsteps of the people proceeding from one side of the house to the other. She wondered which room had the head. She wanted to be the one to find it.

"We don't have much time," Brian said, as the muffled footsteps clomped into another room.

"Oh, you take the study, I'll take the dining room," Michele said uncertainly. Brian ducked under one rope and Michele did the same in the other room.

She tiptoed carefully past a table covered with fragile-looking china. They were really trespassing, she worried, hoping Brian was being careful too. If they accidentally broke something, she guessed their allowance forever would never begin to pay for a priceless antique.

She pulled the small door open just enough to slip inside. She looked down at the floor, assuming the head would be sitting in the corner, maybe in a box or something. But instead of a head, she saw two feet. Michele jumped and looked up at a head and squealed in surprise. "Brian! You scared me to death!"

"You sure you're brave enough to find the pirate's missing head?" he teased.

She could tell he was tickled to have scared her so. "You're in my closet," she admonished.

"No, you're in mine," Brian said, motioning behind him towards the door to the study. "There are two entrances to this chimney room."

"Look," he said, tapping on the window. Below, waving at them were Michael and Jo Dee. Brian made silly faces back at them.

"Hey, remember there are *two* windows in the chimney," Michele said. "Maybe the head is in the closet on the second floor. It just has to be," she added in exasperation.

Again they heard the shuffling of the tour group as they worked their way back down the upstairs hall.

"They're coming back!" Brian said. "How are we going to get upstairs now?"

"Maybe the guide didn't notice that we weren't at the rear of the group," Michele said. "C'mon!"

Quickly they closed the closet doors and slipped back under the ropes into the main hall. They hurried into the parlor and hid on either side of the door just as the tourists started down the staircase. When the last of the group came down, they joined the end of the line and exchanged a relieved smile.

As the guide explained about the restoration of the house, Michele and Brian darted up the stairs. They raced down the hall to the chimney side of the house and each took the corresponding room they had investigated on the first floor.

Michele slipped under the rope of the doorway to a child's bedroom and headed for the closet door beside another huge fireplace.

She hoped she had picked the right room. She really did want to be the one who found the head, she thought. But she would just be glad if it were in one closet or the other this time.

Taking a deep breath, she opened the door. This time she wasn't even a little startled to see Brian standing there, just doubly disappointed.

Brian shook his head, "Nothing here."

Michele picked up a cornhusk broom and swatted a wispy cobweb dangling from the ceiling. "Here either," she said disgustedly. She motioned out the window at the people below. They recognized some of them from the tour group. Michael and Jo Dee were looking anxiously around for them.

"We've got to go down or we'll get locked in," Brian

warned.

"But the head!" Michele said in exasperation.

Brian frowned and shrugged. "What head?"

They each closed their closet doors and scampered down the staircase. The guide was just about to close the heavy front door when they reached the downstairs hall and hurried breathlessly out the door.

"Thought I'd lost you two," the guide said. "Are you coming down into the basement kitchen with us?"

"No thank you," Michele said, "but we enjoyed our tour." It was surely an acting job to say that, she thought.

Michael and Jo Dee came running up. Michael shook his fist at his sister. "You went to the twin chimneys without us," he said.

"Yeah," Jo Dee pouted. "Michael found the note in the bottle and I helped look for the chimneys," she complained.

"Where's the head anyway?" asked Michael.

"Head?" echoed the guide with a concerned look.

Michele gave Michael the skull and crossbones sign but he ignored her and said, "Blackbeard's head in the chimney."

"Oh my goodness!" the guide exclaimed and laughed.

"He's just kidding," Michele said.

"No, I'm . . ." Michael began, then saw Brian's threatening look and hushed.

The guide looked concerned and started to ask Michael more questions. But the tourists were already parading down the stone steps to the kitchen and so the guide indicated she had to leave.

"Let's go to Swindell's and get a drink," said Michael.

"Super," said Jo Dee. "I'm hot and thirsty."

"We'll meet you there in a minute," said Michele as the two vanished into the crowd.

She and Brian wandered dejectedly over to a tree and stretched out in the shade.

"I just don't understand," Michele said. "I know the note in the bottle was sent to us intentionally. And I'm certain we found the right twin chimneys. So why wasn't the head there?"

"Maybe someone else found it first," Brian said.

"That's right!" said Michele. "Maybe they've already returned it to Mr. Tankard."

Brian sat up. "Someone really could have discovered it when they came to clean up and turn on the air conditioning in the Palmer-Marsh house this morning," he said.

Michele nodded. She should be delighted, she thought, but she knew she would be disappointed if anyone except her found the head. She guessed that was her center stage obsession at work again. She wanted to be the heroine and save the show. Oh well, she thought, if someone had found the head and returned it, that would at least resolve part of the mystery — except who took it and why — and maybe that would be enough for the play to go on — *with her in it.*

She jumped up and brushed the loose grass from the back of her jeans. "There's only one way to find out — let's go to the ticket office."

As they approached the small brick building on Water Street with its black and white glossy photos of different scenes from the play in the window, Michele suddenly felt excited.

"That surely must be what happened," she said to Brian. "A caretaker found the head and returned it and . . ."

". . . and you can be in the play," Brian finished for her. "I sure hope so — then we can quit this wild goose chase and eat lunch. Besides, I wish I could see you stumble around up there forgetting your lines," he teased.

Just the very thought gave her cold goosebumps of excitement on her hot, perspiring arms.

"I hope you get your . . ." she began as Brian opened the door and she followed him inside. But as she said "wish," she knew her wishes had just vanished once more.

There stood Mr. Tankard, pale as a ghost, staring down into an open metal box on the counter. He looked up at them and said in a hoarse whisper, "I don't believe it . . . it's all gone!"

9 A Gross Black Hair

They could easily see that the small metal box could not possibly hold a big, bushy head. But it was obvious from the dismay on Mr. Tankard's face that whatever the box had contained was as important to him as the head was to them.

"What was in the box, sir?" Michele asked.

Mr. Tankard stared blankly at them. Freckles of perspiration dotted his pink cheeks. The pouches beneath his eyes sagged sadly.

"Children," he began in a serious tone. "In this box was the ticket money for the opening week performances — over $2,000." A bubble of perspiration dripped off one of the old man's eyebrows and fell into the empty box with a soft ping.

"I came to get the money and take it to the bank in Washington. Then I was coming back to write payroll checks."

"Wow! Who do you think got it?" asked Brian.

"I guess whoever's been causing all this mischief," Mr. Tankard said. "It's been relatively minor things till now, but this is a treacherous blow to the drama."

"What will you do?" Michele asked fearfully.

"I guess if we can't pay the cast and crew, they won't perform. You can't blame them," he added forlornly.

"Oh, please don't give up," Michele pleaded. "Maybe the police can find the money. Maybe whoever took it will return it. Maybe the cast will at least start the play while we, I mean they, look for the money," Michele spouted breathlessly, trying to concoct a happy conclusion to this new tragedy.

"I'm afraid it takes more than *maybes* to keep a play going, young lady," Mr. Tankard said. "You youngsters run along, and I'll call the police so they can search for this scandalous pirate!"

The very word *pirate* gave Michele an angry chill. So did the sudden creak of the door behind them. They turned and there stood John, hands on hips, looking aggravated as the dickens.

"You kids missed lunch," he said sternly. "If you don't check in more often, I'll have to limit your galavanting."

Just as though he'd never said a word, both of them burst into an animated explanation that the money from the play had been stolen.

As Michele reached to tilt the empty box toward him in proof, she spotted something. She gently shifted the hinge that had been pried open. Slowly, she pulled a long coarse hair through the lock. It was black.

"Let me see," said John, taking it from her. Michele carefully handed it to him, then wiped her hands on the seat of her jeans.

"This could very well be evidence," said John. "You kids run on back to the motel now and let Tank and me get the law over here."

"Aw, phooey," said Brian.

Mr. Tankard was still sweating and shaking. Michele could tell John was worried that Mr. Tankard was so upset that he might have a heart attack or something. She hoped John had taken a C.P.R. course like her Mother had. They sure didn't need any more problems. She wanted to stay but knew it would be best if they left so John could calm Tank down.

Reluctantly Michele trudged out the door and followed Brian down Water Street into the steamy sunshine. Holding her forefinger and thumb pressed tightly together, Michele put her hand near Brian's face.

"The hair!" he said. "But I saw you give it to John."

"I broke about a third of it off real quick," she explained. "I figured this gross old hair just might be a clue."

Brian looked at her with admiration. Carefully, he took the strand from her. "It's just as coarse as can be."

"Do you think it's off a real head or a costume head?" asked Michele.

"The police lab could tell," Brian said with a wistful glance back at the ticket office.

As they walked along silently mulling the mystery over in their minds, they became aware of a clomp-clomp behind them coming closer and closer until the sound seemed to echo in their ears. They turned and saw the tall, bearded figure striding toward them in his high, mud-encrusted boots. The canvas sack hung from his hand and seemed to drag on the ground with its weight.

The figure strode brusquely past them as though they were invisible. The bushy black head never looked up as the man made the same turn by the Buzzard Inn he had the day before and disappeared.

Brian stopped sharp and held the hair aloft against the sky.

"It could be," he said.

"He's certainly acting suspiciously," Michele said. "And his hair looks like a few million of these all tangled together," she added, squinting at the single strand that almost looked like a rope against the blue sky. "We've just got to find out who he is and what's in that sack."

They caught up with Jo Dee and Michael at Swindell's Store and told them what had happened as they herded them toward the motel. "Let's go swimming!" Michael squealed as he spotted the public pier jutting out into the bay.

Michele looked out at the blue-gray water with its mini-whitecaps twinkling. "We might as well do something to pass the time till John gets back," she said.

They had put their swimsuits on under their clothes that morning. Racing down the pier, they tossed tee shirts and tennis shoes all along the weather-beaten boards until they each reached the end and disappeared into the cool, blue bay with a splash.

The next morning Bath was buzzing early with news of the theft. A blue police car cruised around the tiny town.

Cast members wandered forlornly around the ticket office as though their paychecks might float down from the sky.

Fortunately, Michele thought, everyone was too busy to pay any attention to four children huddled under a fir tree by the water's edge. Michael had awakened first and raced down to the creek. Now he sat proudly in the center of the others holding a dripping brown bottle in his hands.

"Let me open it," Brian said impatiently, but Michael continued to pick determinedly at the cork.

"Hurry it up brother," Michele urged.

Jo Dee giggled nervously. The cork spurted from the bottle's neck with a wet hiss. The roll of paper inside was twisted tightly and slipped right out. Brian grabbed it greedily and unrolled it.

"Let me read it," said Michael, snatching the note away. "You can't read yet!" Michele said.

"Oh, yes I can!" he mumbled and handed the note back to Brian.

"Somebody read it!" insisted Michele.

10 A Mysterious New Clue

Brian cleared his throat and read in a deep voice, as the writer might have while scrawling out the clue:

"So you think the chimneys were a dead end. . .
Remember – Blackbeard's head hung in the wind."

"Yuck!" Jo Dee said, and Michele could tell from the look on her face that she was vividly picturing that scene.

"That's a good clue and a bad clue," Michael said.

"What do you mean?" asked Brian.

"Well at least we're not at a dead end — anyway, I hope not," she said, as the police car slowly passed the motel. "But the second line could mean anything — it doesn't tell us where to look."

"That's true," agreed Brian. "The head could be hanging in the wind anywhere. Remember that when Blackbeard was killed at Ocracoke, they swung his head from the bowsprit of the ship and they threw the body in Teach's Hole."

"Is the head we're looking for at Ocracoke, where Blackbeard was killed?" asked Michael.

"Oh, I sure hope not," said Michele, alarmed at the very thought. "But the clue does mean the head could be hanging almost anywhere. What we need is to know more about

Blackbeard than was in the play."

"Well you know what Mom does when she wants to know something," Michael volunteered.

"Exactly!" said Michele. "Super idea Michael!"

"What?" asked Jo Dee and Brian together.

"When she has to write something that she doesn't know a lot about she researches first at the library," explained Michele. "You do have a library in Bath?"

"Of course," said Jo Dee.

"As a matter of fact," added Brian, "when Bath was just a frontier settlement, a library of 1,000 books was given to St. Thomas Parish. It was the first public library in North Carolina."

"Well, what are we waiting for?" asked Michael.

"You to put your clothes on," said Jo Dee laughing.

"Yo ho ho!" Michael jumped up. "Wait for me!"

The Bath Public Library was nestled between a run-down, vacant house and the St. Thomas Parish Church. Inside was one large room with thick carpet you could sprawl out on to read, a fireplace, a seashell display, and shelves and shelves of books.

Michele knew this would be a great place to spend a rainy day, at least when she wasn't trying to solve a mystery. In the center of the room was a big black desk. Behind it sat a tiny, white-haired woman.

"Good morning, children," the librarian greeted them in a whispery voice. "Make yourselves at home. Look around all you want."

Michele thought the woman seemed delighted to have kids come in to read. Since there was no one else in the library, it looked like she could use some customers.

"Do you have a summer reading program?" Michele asked. She had gotten a certificate for reading ten books during the summer vacation every year since she'd been old enough to read. Of course, she usually read twice that many at least, not even counting the books she read to Michael.

"Certainly," the woman said, rising from her chair. "Can I find you a copy of *Little Women*, or the delightful *Huckleberry Finn*?"

Michele had read both of these two or three times each and so she shook her head *no*.

Brian said, "What we want . . . See, we found this . . ."

". . . this map," Michele burst in. She knew it wouldn't be good to get an adult suspicious about floating bottles, although she wondered if anyone would really believe them if they told.

"A map?" the woman said, rubbing one bony hand over the other. "We have lots of maps, atlases, encyclopedias . . ."

"No ma'm," Michele said politely. "I mean we found this map and some information about Bath at the Center and so we're interested in some local history . . . like about pirates — Blackbeard, maybe."

"Aha, the drama sparked your curiosity!" the librarian said and grinned. "Not surprised . . . not surprised . . . not surprised at anything these days, especially all the mysterious goin's on surrounding the play. That sparks *my* imagination, and my ire."

Michael looked up from a Dr. Seuss Book — *The Cat in the Hat*. Michele hoped he wouldn't get that one. It was super, but she bet she had read it a million times to him. Well, almost that many times. She just knew he had looked up to see what the librarian's "ire" was.

"Makes me angry, all these goin's on," she continued, flapping her skeletal fingers up and down agitatedly. "No peace and quiet in town ever since they started all this historic site stuff."

Michele sighed, and sat down in one of the armchairs. If everyone felt that way we wouldn't have any of our heritage left for people to see, she thought sadly.

"Blackbeard," the librarian said, as though she suddenly remembered why the children had come in. "Blackbeard's been the pirate king of stage spectaculars on Broadway in New York City and penny-plain-tuppence-coloured-cardboard theatres too."

Michele laughed at the unusual description of a theater. At this point she would settle for being in a penny-plain-play. But maybe they could get a clue here so she wouldn't have to settle for less than being in Bath's outdoor drama.

Brian dumped a stack of books in Michele's lap, and gave her the skull and crossbones sign.

"Can we take these outside under the trees and look at them?" Michele asked. "And let the little ones read in here?" she added in a motherly tone. She could hear Brian groan under his breath at her play-acting. But it worked, she thought, biting her tongue so she wouldn't get tickled.

Frizzy white curls bobbed up and down as the librarian nodded her head.

Michele and Brian glided quickly toward the door and outside. "It's too hot to sit in the glebe. Let's sit over here."

Now it was Michele's turn to look around for something

she didn't know what was.

Brian laughed. "That's the glebe," he said, pointing to the house next door to the library. The paint was peeling off the walls in big, ugly blotches.

"Could have fooled me," Michele said, determined not to ask what she hoped he would volunteer.

"A glebe was land set aside by the Lord Proprietors to encourage a minister to settle here," Brian explained.

"Why don't they paint it and fix it up?" Michele asked.

"Money, of course," said Brian. "Most people don't know how expensive it is to renovate these old places."

"My Mom has a lot of friends who've remodeled old townhouses in downtown Raleigh and Savannah and Richmond, and they brag about what a bargain it was," Michele argued.

"Yeah," said Brian, "it might be to paint and put up wallpaper. But that's just remodeling. When they renovate or restore these houses they put them back as close to the original as they can. That's expensive — finding old molding, or researching old wallpaper patterns."

"I see what you mean," Michele said, realizing that there was more than met the eye to sharing historic sites.

She followed Brian to the St. Thomas Cemetery and sat down beside him on an overturned tombstone. It was almost like twilight under the low-hanging fir trees, which smelled strangely like Christmas in the hot sun that glistened in their top branches. But in the shade the tombstone felt like a block of ice against the backs of her legs.

For a few minutes, they silently thumbed through the

indexes in the back of the books. They both found the pages they were looking for and began reading aloud together at the same time.

"Blackbeard . . ."

Michele laughed, "You go first."

"No," said Brian, "you're the one with the script reading practice."

"Ha!" said Michele. "Unless we find that head there won't be any reason for me to read a script. But maybe one of these books will at least give us a clue to the clue."

They read for awhile, but nothing seemed to relate to the clue in the bottle.

Michele slammed her book in disgust. "Let's forget it a minute," she suggested. "When Mom has to come up with an idea, she puts all the info she can in her head and tells herself what she needs to come up with. Then she forgets about it, and later the answer comes to her."

"That's weird," Brian said.

"She says that's the way creativity works. Your brain's like a computer. You put the data in and ask it a question, and it does its thing and spits the answer back out at you."

"Well let's go inside the church and cool off while we're creating," Brian said.

As they entered the dim sanctuary, Brian told her, "This is the oldest church building in North Carolina still in existence. They've held church services here for 240 years."

Michele stooped down and rubbed her palm over the cold floor which had faded traces of decorations on the red tiles.

"The tiles used to be embedded in sand so they could

remove them," said Brian. "They buried settlers underneath so the Indians wouldn't find them."

Brian giggled as Michele snatched her hand away. They walked side by side down the center aisle toward the shadowy altar.

Brian was telling her that the candelabra was said to have been given to the church by King George II, when he stopped short and looked like he'd seen a ghost.

"What is it?" begged Michele.

"Look!" Brian said, pointing to the altar.

In spooky St. Thomas Church

11 Pirate In A Graveyard

Michele gasped. The collection plate was filled with money. The mound of bills had even spilled over onto the altar and floor.

"That's some love offering," said Michele.

"That's no love offering," said Brian, scooping up a handful of money from the floor.

Michele looked at him, puzzled. "What is it then?" she asked.

"That," he said, letting the handful of dollars trickle through his fingers and fall back into the plate, "is the missing ticket money."

Without talking, they quickly stuffed the bills between the pages of their books and hurried back down the aisle. Just as Michele was ready to follow Brian out the door, she turned to make sure they had not dropped any money. Through the glass of the windows, she felt certain she saw the shaggy shadow of a hairy head.

Several nights later, Michele sat on the edge of the deck staring morosely out at the flashing red buoy light in the bay. Everyone had been delighted when they returned the money and agreed opening night should go on after all. But there was still the mystery of the missing head, and until it was solved, John would not let them participate in any of the theater activities.

Brian came out and sat down beside her. "Well, have you had any creative brainstorms yet?"

Michele shrugged her shoulders. Here they had a new clue since early morning and had made absolutely no progress in figuring out what it meant. "Blank. I'll just have to think about it a little longer," she said, knowing that now that the play would be underway, every day was one less she could have been part of it.

She watched the gray dusk fall around her. Inside she felt just as blah. The deck seemed like an empty stage after a play with all the make-believe unmade. In the distance she could hear a faint bell ringing irregularly, as though blown by the wind. Suddenly, she sat upright.

"What?" Brian asked. "Did it come to you?"

"Maybe," she said excitedly. "Can a bell *blow in the wind* — like it said in the clue?"

"Sure," he said.

"Where is there a bell in Bath?" she asked.

Brian hung his head in thought. "Only the fire bell . . . no, of course! There's Queen Anne's Bell. It's even older that the Liberty Bell."

"Where is it?" Michele asked.

"In St. Thomas Cemetery," Brian said. "In fact, Michael and Jo Dee were pulling on the rope when they were playing tag the other day."

"But I didn't hear it ring?" Michele said.

"Maybe there was something stuffed in it that kept it from

ringing," Brian said slowly.

They exchanged *could-it-be* looks. "Let's go see!" Michele said, then paused. "Won't John and the kids miss us?"

"I don't think so," said Brian. "They're watching a movie, and you know how John usually falls asleep in his chair when he watches TV anyway."

"Well, I know I don't want to watch some of that silly stuff they have on TV," Michele said. "I'd rather be living out an adventure than watching someone else do it on the tube. So let's go!"

They tiptoed across the deck, stooping to crawl beneath John's window, then slipped down the side steps. Tideriggings followed. They took every shortcut they could. No one seemed to be outside.

Beneath the fir trees the graveyard was almost as black as the bottom of the sea. Even the moon couldn't beam much light between the thickly woven branches.

The church looked spooky at night. In the darkness, the tumbled tombstones looked like a vampire had knocked them over in his hurry to get away for the evening. Michele shivered, remembering that Blackbeard was supposed to be buried someplace around Bath.

"Where's the bell?" she whispered.

"Follow me," Brian urged, weaving through the marble markers and around the trees as though he were sneaking up on the small bell house near the center of the churchyard. He had to feel for the rope to recall which corner of the roof the bell was anchored in. Grasping the knotted end, he tugged gently, but there was no sound.

"Pull hard!" Michele urged.

He gave the rope a yank but there was still no noise. Michele stuck her head under the shed and looked up in the dark corner but could see nothing. Brian jerked the rope again. Suddenly, a mass of coarse matter fell down upon their heads.

They both cried out and ducked, frantically pulling the stiff fibers from their hair.

Brian stooped down and picked up a handful of the wiry strands. "Pinestraw! It's not a head – it's a bird's nest. That's why the bell didn't ring!"

"*Another* dead end, another useless clue," Michele said, discouraged. "It's like we're being led to the head, but they really don't want us to find it."

"Hush!" Brian said suddenly, grabbing her shoulder and pulling her close to the ground.

Michele looked up from the puddle of pinestraw to see what had silenced Brian. Coming across the churchyard she could see the outline of a huge figure. Michele thought it either had a pointed ear or was wearing a tricorn type of hat. Full sleeves and big-kneed britches billowed from the figure. On one side, a sash flowed as it swayed toward them. On the other side, a stiff pointed object like a sword clanged with each nearing step.

Suddenly, the figure stopped and turned sideways toward the church. Michele and Brian gasped. From the front you couldn't see it, but in silhouette from the side the ragged outline of a massive beard was obvious. A monstrous hand drew the sword which glistened like a silver spear in the night.

In a silent signal Brian gripped Michele's shoulder again so tightly it hurt. They both jumped up and ran as fast as they could, stumbling over tombstones and tree roots. Tideriggings followed, barking wildly. Neither of them stopped or looked back until they reached the safety of the streetlights on Water Street.

The figure bellowed at them, but its deep voice was garbled by the wind.

"*Who* was that?" asked Brian, breathlessly.

"I don't know," Michele answered, "but he had a bushy head."

"Let's go back to the motel and watch TV awhile," Brian said.

Michele nodded, and glancing over her shoulder, she raced as fast as she could for the Harbor Light.

12 THE STRANGE SIGN CHANGE

The next morning a squawking Fuzzbucket awoke Michele from her tossing and turning. Her head hurt from dreaming a series of chasing, getting-caught, getting-away dreams. She felt exhausted and not ready to hear about anymore crises from the three kids standing at the foot of her bed.

"Michael! Move that drippy bottle," she grumbled.

"It's a clue," Michael told her.

"Big deal," Michele said, feeling ill at her brother and more ill at herself for taking it out on him.

"Sorry, Mike," she added, reaching for the limp note he held out to her. She yawned. Rubbing the sleep from the corners of her eyes, she read the clue in a mumbled monotone:

"If not finding the head is what you fear,
You'd better check out the Vand . . . "

"What the heck does this mean?" Michele asked irritably. "The rest of the word is washed away. It's just a smear of blue ink." She tossed the note back at them.

"We know what it means!" Jo Dee squealed. "At least Brian does."

Michele rubbed her tangled hair. The top of her head felt like a pile of pinestraw and she wasn't sure she liked Brian

81

seeing her all messy. He just stood there in his neat jeans and tee shirt looking smart.

"Oh, all right," she grumbled. "I give up. What does it mean?"

"Well," said Brian, "I thought at first *Vand* might be the beginning of the word "Vandyke" which is a pointy kind of beard like the artist Van Gogh wore."

Michele yawned again and stretched back on her pillow as though she were bored and could doze off. "I know that," she barked.

Brian sighed and turned on his heels. "C'mon, kids, let's leave Sleeping Ugly alone and start on this clue ourselves."

"Wait!" Michele said, sitting upright. "I'm sorry. My head just hurts," she said, rubbing it dramatically as evidence.

"Throbs — or *rings*?" Brian asked with a smile.

"Clangs like a bell," Michele said, grinning back at him. "Tell me about the clue."

"Well, Vandyke and beard seem to go together, but what the word really means is Van Der Veer," Brian said proudly.

"Is that a kind of beard too?" asked Michael.

"No, it's the newest addition to the historic houses," Brian explained. "It was built at Catnip Point around 1790."

"But that's where the amphitheater is," Michele said.

"You're right," Brian said. "But they moved the Van Der Veer house. It's next to the Center now."

"I didn't even notice it before," Michele said. "I thought it looked like some of the newer homes going up in Raleigh, but I guess architects and builders copy these traditional designs. Can we get inside?"

"I don't know," said Brian, "but I think we should take a walk over there anyway, just to see."

"Yeah," agreed Jo Dee.

"Let's go!" said Michael, waving the bottle in the air.

"Wait for me downstairs," Michele said, bouncing out of bed, her headache forgotten.

They stopped at the Pirate's Treasure to say good morning to Ben. He was busy unpacking crates of glass mugs with Blackbeard's picture on them. Michele knew the theater was trying anything to make money for the play.

"You two were right smart to find that missing ticket money," Ben said. "Just happened to luck up on it, hey," he teased. "Any luck with the head yet?"

"No luck at all, but . . ." Michele began, then stopped when she saw Brian make "the sign."

Ben laughed. "Better hurry up. Be time for opening night before long. By the way," Ben added with a wink, "I was looking out my window about midnight last night and could'a swore I saw you two running in and out of the shadows like a pirate was chasing you."

"*Us?*" said Brian, with a nervous laugh.

"You know John wouldn't let us be out that late," Michele assured him in her best acting manner. "Why he'd restrict us for a week," she added for good measure.

"Not if he didn't know . . . not if he didn't know!" Ben bellowed at them.

Michele herded the younger kids toward the door. Brian waved good-bye and followed them as fast as he could.

They must have walked around the two-story Van Der Veer house a hundred times when Michele sat down in disgust and said, "It's no use, we can't get in till it opens."

Michael and Jo Dee had given up long ago. They had brought the bottle and clue along and were playing "drop the mystery clue in the bottle." As far as Michele was concerned, they might as well drop it back in the ocean.

Brian sprawled in the shade against the house, his eyes looking as though his thoughts were far away. He finally spoke.

"I'm beginning to see what your Mother means."

"What do *you* mean?" Michele asked.

"My creative computer of a brain just remembered something. Since the Van Der Veer house was moved here from Catnip Point, maybe the clue didn't mean the *house*, but the *homeplace*. When most people around here talk about things or places, they always mean where it originally was or named for. Like the Jones Place would be called that no matter who moved in or out of it, just because the Joneses built it."

"We looked at the amphitheater once," Michele said.

"Well, let's look again. We're overlooking something somewhere," Brian said. "And if we don't get back for breakfast, John will be looking all over for us."

As they walked back to the motel, they could smell the bacon John was frying. Everybody was starving.

"I believe I'm going to have to fry the whole hog before we can get through the meal," John joked. Even Jo Dee had her plate out for seconds.

Their spirits improved when John suggested they attend the play's opening that night in support of the cast.

John had a list of chores for each of them and so it was after dinner and time for the play before they even got a chance to get to Catnip Point.

They arrived at the amphitheater in time to watch a beautiful Bath sunset. Out over the bay a swollen orange sun sank slowly into the purple water. When sun and water met, the world seemed to explode into plum and peach fireworks.

As soon as all the leftover slivers of sunshine sank into the bay, they hurried to get popcorn and a good seat.

"Where is everyone?" Michele asked, as they surveyed the nearly empty parking area. "It's almost curtain time. Do you think people thought we wouldn't have a performance?"

"It's been on all the radio stations and papers that the show would go on," John said. "Maybe there was some traffic around Washington, or the ferry was late."

Michele wandered down an outside aisle of the amphitheater. Some of the cast were peeking out from behind the black curtains, and Michele knew they must be wondering where everyone was.

Only a handful of people were scattered in the audience when it was curtain time. Michele noticed that most of them seemed to be local people. Maybe out-of-towners had heard some rumor that the play was canceled and so had not bothered to come, Michele thought. It would be awful if they had a poor turnout, or if anyone wanted a refund on their ticket money.

As the lights dimmed and an actor came out to read the

prologue, Michele forgot about the problems of the play and the people, and even about looking for the head, and became absorbed in the drama. She could just imagine herself playing a leading role, and yet more and more the possibility seemed just a dream.

When the lights came on at intermission, she was surprised to see the audience almost full. Mr. Tankard came up the stage steps to speak to the cast. Michele grabbed his coat sleeve as he passed her seat. "Where did everyone come from?" she asked.

"Someone changed the road sign at the fork in Washington. They turned the Bath sign towards Swan Quarter. That made everyone follow the wrong road. Some are irritated and want their money back. Seems like this play is just doomed, Michele, doomed," he said, shaking his head in frustration.

"Oh brother," said Michele. "What in the world else can happen?"

"I don't know," Brian said as the lights dimmed for the second act. "But from the look on Tank's face, if we don't solve this mystery soon, this play and your chances of being in it are sunk like a pirate ship."

13 A HOUSEFUL OF CLUES

When Michele came downstairs for breakfast the next morning, she was surprised and delighted to find Mother having coffee with John.

"Mother! You didn't tell us you were coming!" Michele said and squeezed her Mom's neck so hard the coffee sloshed over the rim of her cup into the saucer.

"Not so dramatic!" Mother said, squeezing back just as tightly. "I had to come to Greenville to pick up some sketches and couldn't resist coming on down to see everyone. Is everything ok?"

"I'm getting old and gray trying to keep up with them," John teased with a wink.

"Things are fine," Michele said. "We've learned a lot about Bath and pirates and have been swimming a lot, and they have the neatest little library here, but . . ." Michele stopped and slumped down in a heap on the floor by her Mother's feet.

". . . but they haven't found that missing head yet?" Mother finished.

"Exactly!" Michele said. "Just finding that stupid old head would solve everything, and I would have a chance to be in a real play before I'm old and gray."

"Such ambition!" said Mother. "I was delighted to get

published before I was thirty. But I guess your reach should exceed your grasp."

"It seems like my grasp has been at straws so far this summer," Michele said.

A quizzical two-plus-two-equals-four look came over John's face. "Just how hard have you kids been looking for that head?" he asked.

"Oh . . ." Michele began, biting her tongue for saying too much. "We've just been keeping our eyes open."

"Hm, I think I'd better keep *my* eyes open," John said, winking at Mother again. "Lash them to the yardarms!"

"Now, who's acting," Mother said and laughed. She stroked Michele's hair. "There's always next year," she said reassuringly.

Mother and John went on talking about the latest events surrounding the drama when Michele spied something on the deck. Another small brown bottle was perched on the bottom rail. The sun shone straight through the amber glass and Michele could tell the bottle was empty.

Darn, she thought. Those kids have found a new clue and left me behind. She could just see Brian strutting down the street swinging Blackbeard's head. How dare he upstage her! She shouldn't care who found it at this point, but she always did want to be the star of the show, as Mother said. Was that so bad? She just wanted to be special, to stand out from the crowd. She would too, doggone it, she thought, watching Tideriggings pace back and forth on the deck as though he were guarding the bottle.

She had to get outside and hide the bottle before Mother

and John spotted it. They probably wouldn't think it was a mystery clue bottle, but they sure might think it was a beer bottle, and that would take as much explaining.

Michele stretched and yawned. "Think I'll get dressed and go for a walk," she said, standing around and heading towards the door.

As she was leaving, Mother said, "Honey, you can worry about that head all you want, but it isn't going to do much good from what John has been telling me."

Michele turned and looked at John.

"Tank's about had it," he said. "Everyone has. Box office receipts were down last night because of the tampering with the road sign." John shook his head slowly. "They're going to run through this weekend, but it's pretty certain Tankard will shut down for the season on Sunday night unless we have some miracle between now and then."

Michele felt near tears. Not only for herself, but also for the people who had worked so hard to start the drama, and for the town.

Mother spoke to John, but looked at Michele. "I guess that means they wouldn't even attempt to have the play next season?"

"That's probably right," said John. "Not with as much trouble as they've had this year."

"Oh, Mother!" Michele said.

"I'm afraid every drama doesn't have a happy ending in real life," Mother said.

That's for sure, Michele thought as she went outside. But she wasn't a character in a play with a script to go by. She still had time to rewrite the ending of this drama!

Michele grumbled to herself as she jogged down Water Street. No one was at the Center. The ticket office was closed so the kids weren't there. She peeked in the library window but only saw the top of the librarian's head behind her sand dune of books.

Discouraged, Michele wandered on down Water Street to Bonner's Point. She could sure see why Captain Bonner had built his house on the edge of the glistening blue bay. The view of Plum Point was just beautiful.

She turned away from the bay and took a shortcut across the Bonner yard. It looked like some of the country inns she had seen around North Carolina. Sunlight sprinkled the side of the house, glistening in the windows.

Suddenly, Michele looked, then looked again, startled. There was a face in the upstairs window. Another appeared. And another. The faces were distorted through the rippled glass panes. When the bobbing heads got still she could see it was the kids!

She ran to the front porch and up the steps. Suddenly, the door opened. An arm reached out, grabbed her by the wrist and yanked her inside. "Ouch!" Michele said. "Don't be so rough, you traitors."

But the three kids just stood there, their eyes gleaming as though they knew the best secret in the world.

"Hey," she said, more suspicious than ever. She could feel their unexplained excitement. "What gives? I saw the bottle — what did the note say?"

"It was written in a big hurry," Michael said excitedly.

Sneaking up the staircase

"Like a right-handed person writing with their left," Jo Dee added.

"It only said *Bonner House*," Michael said.

"You were asleep and the clue seemed so vague that we just thought we'd come on over and look around," Brian apologized.

Michele gave him an unforgiving look. "How did you get in?"

"The cleaning man was here. We slipped in the back door while he was vacuuming and he never even heard us," Brian said.

"That's trespassing," Michele said, knowing she would have done the same thing. "You'll get in big trouble."

She was sorry she'd said that when she saw the worried look on Michael and Jo Dee's faces.

"Well, we could leave," Brian said. "But I don't think you'll want to," he added confidently.

"Why?" Michele asked, her insides quivering with excitement. "Have you found the head?"

"No!" Michael volunteered. "But there are clues *everywhere*. We must be getting close this time."

"Clues everywhere?" Michele repeated.

"We think so, anyway," Jo Dee clarified.

"A second note was stuck in the door knocker," explained Brian, "saying to '*look hard*'. And when Michael was running upstairs, he spotted another piece of paper on a door."

"What did it say?" Michele begged, holding her head with her hands, hardly believing a house full of clues.

Michael gave her the note he had just found. Michele read quickly:

"You'll find the head.
Today's the day.
Let the lustre light the way."

"Boy, I sure wish we'd toured this house earlier, so I'd know what the lustre is," Michele said.

"If we don't figure it out fast, it will be time for the tours to start," Brian warned. "We've got to find the head before then."

"I know what the lustre is," Jo Dee said quietly.

"Aw c'mon, Dee," Brian said, "how would you know?"

"I toured the house one day with my class," she said. She pointed to a small table by the stairs. "That's a lustre."

They all moved closer to the table and admired the carousel of glass prisms hanging fragilely from a center piece of glass.

"What in the world?" said Michele. "In colonial days everything was very practical and had some purpose, but this doesn't seem to do anything but sit there and look pretty."

"That's right," said Jo Dee excitedly. "That's what the guide told us. You put it where the sun shines on it and it looks pretty."

"Hey," Brian said, "she's right! If the sun shines through those prisms, the light will refract and should shine toward a particular direction — and *point the way*!"

"Well, it can't possibly get any light unless we move it out of that dark corner," said Michele.

"We could put it in the middle of the hall," said Michael, pointing to a spot where the morning sun was streaming in through the hall windows.

Carefully, Michele lifted the lustre, trying not to think that it was probably irreplaceable. The glass pieces tinkled softly against one another as she walked slowly to the spot Michael had indicated. Even more carefully, she handed the lustre to Brian. He placed it in a fat puddle of sunshine on the floor. When the sun entered the glass prisms, it spewed back out again in multi-colored streaks like sunshine rainbows across the dark wooden floor.

"It's beautiful," said Jo Dee, stooping and turning the lustre gently. The streaks of sunlight shattered into confetti fireworks on the creamy walls.

They watched the prisms play with the light. Michael's eyes followed the longest streak of light across the floor and up the side of the grandfather clock. "There!" he said, pointing to the glass-covered face. Just then the clock chimed four hollow rings.

14 IF YOU HAVE THE GUTS

"It isn't four o'clock," Michael complained.

"It just chimes when it takes a notion," Joe Dee explained. "The guide said it always has."

"Wonder what made it take a notion just now?" Michael muttered under his breath.

Brian had already gone to the clock and was pulling a small slip of white paper from the rim of the door.

"Read! Read!" they all clamored at him.

"Then hush," said Brian, nervously, unfolding the note.

"Don't be a fool . . .
Look in the pontipool."

Brian looked at Michele and shrugged. Michele shook her head back at him. They both looked at Jo Dee. Here they were on the verge of finding the head, Michele pondered, and they were at the mercy of a ten-year-old. "Have you got that item covered?" she asked Jo Dee, hopefully.

Jo Dee tossed her head cockily. "Sure," she said in delight. "Follow me."

They traipsed single file behind her into the parlor. She pointed out a flowered metal pot surrounded by tea cups.

Carefully, Michele opened the lid and began to take the

insides of the pontipool apart.

"It's like an old-fashioned coffee pot," Michael said.

"They made tea in it," explained Jo Dee.

"There's no clue in here," Michele said.

Michael reached out and pulled a small drawer in the base of the container. Like a jack-in-the-box, a white slip of paper popped up.

"Good work, Michael," Michele said, reading aloud:

"Go straight to the bedroom . . .
Don't walk . . . run fast,
You just might see a head in the glass."

They all ran out of the parlor together, almost overturning the lustre that was still sitting on the hall floor.

Michele could feel her nerve endings tingle with each twinkle of the rattling glass. "Wait!" she ordered. "We've got to put this up."

With a clattery jangle she and Jo Dee returned the lustre to the table, then tore up the stairs after the boys.

Suddenly, Michael, who was leading the way tripped, sprawling across the upstairs landing. His face turned red.

Jo Dee laughed, "It must work!" she said.

"What works?" Michael groaned, rubbing his knee.

"The guide said this little top step was shorter than the rest so that when the men came in late at night from the tavern they would trip and fall and wake up their wife who would know how late it was."

"Good idea," said Michele. "I think some new homes

could use those."

"Funny!" said Brian. "It sounds like a sneaky trick to me."

"Let's hope this clue's not another trick," Michele said, helping her brother up.

Since the corner bedroom was the largest, they began their search there. "What are we looking for?" Brian asked.

"A glass," Michael repeated from the clue. "A face in the glass."

They each took a window and were silent as they looked carefully over every pane.

"Nothing," Brian grumbled. "This is like a scavenger hunt, except we're not finding anything but more clues."

"It is beginning to seem like a make-believe mystery," Michele agreed. "I feel like Alice in Wonderland with all her instructions to do this and do that and off with her head. Hey that's it!" she said, interrupting herself.

"It's what?" the others pleaded.

"Alice-through-the-looking-glass," she said. "We're not looking for a window — we're looking for a mirror. Jo Dee?" she asked hopefully.

"Right!" responded Jo Dee triumphantly, going to a small table and picking up a brass object.

"That's no mirror," said Michael. "There's no glass."

"It's a sailor's mirror," explained Jo Dee. "Glass might break on a ship so they had brass mirrors. See for yourself," she said, handing the mirror to Michele.

Michele stared into the shiny oval at her bronze reflection. It was sort of like looking into a puddle of gold water, she thought. "I can see myself," she agreed, turning toward them.

The others gasped. "And we can see the next clue," Brian said. "It's taped on the back."

He ripped the white slip off and read:

"As in any treasure hunt,
X marks the spots."

"Weird," said Michael. "Why does it say spots? You have only one X spot in a treasure hunt."

"I don't know what that clue means," Jo Dee said disappointedly. "This mystery seems to have lots of X's and no spots."

"Let's look all around the room," Brian suggested. "If there's another note we might find it."

The others searched frantically but Michele sat dejectedly on the side of the plump featherbed. She was beginning to believe that someone wanted to keep them occupied indefinitely. "We could fill up this case with our useless clues," she said, fumbling with a china container on the bedside table. The lid slipped off and out popped another slip of paper, along with several small, sticky black circles. "Spots . . . beauty spots!" she cried.

Michael climbed out from under the bed and inspected the black spot on the tip of his sister's finger. "They look like ugly spots to me," he said.

"Ladies used to wear these on their face to be pretty," Michele said.

Jo Dee pressed her finger to Michele's and carefully plastered the spot on her cheek. She picked up the brass mirror and looked at her distorted image.

"It looks like somebody squashed a tick on your face," Michael said.

Jo Dee yanked the spot off and threw it at him but it stuck on the end of her finger which made everyone howl, except for Michele. She sat silently rereading the note. It was probably the best clue they had so far, she thought.

"I think we've really got it this time," she whispered. "At least the head truly could be in the next spot. It surely could," she repeated.

"What does it say?" Michael asked in an even softer whisper than his sister's.

They all drew closer and Michele read slowly and dramatically in a voice as deep as she supposed the writer of the notes might be.

"I am tired, the hunt is over,
Find it, I don't care.
If you have the guts, the stomach,
Open the trunk that's under the stair."

"Let's go back downstairs fast and see!" said Michael.

"Noooo," stuttered Jo Dee.

"Aw, you don't have to look if you're scared," Brian chided her.

"No!" she repeated stubbornly. "The trunk isn't under the big staircase, it's under the steps to the attic. The guide said it's the only piece original to the house."

"What does that mean?" asked Michael. "Like the original recipe?"

"That means it's the only piece of furniture that was already in the house when they first opened it up to restore it," Michele said.

"We'd better look fast," Brian urged, motioning out the window. "Here comes the guide with the first tour of the day. If she finds us here, we'll be in big trouble."

Michele thought of John's remark that morning about lashing them to the yardarm. "You better believe it," she agreed, scrambling off the bed.

"How are we ever going to get a bloody head out of here without anyone seeing it?" Michael asked. Jo Dee squealed.

"It's not bloody," Michele reassured her. "It's pretend, remember."

They hurried across the hall. Underneath the narrow staircase to the attic, there sat a small deerskin trunk.

"Does the guide usually open it?" Michele asked, worried they were in for another disappointment.

"No," said Jo Dee. "She said it was too old and fragile to open safely."

Together they huddled by the trunk. Michele grasped the clasp. The lid pulled loose easily, as though it had been opened recently, in spite of what Jo Dee said. The words to the clue appeared in her mind in giant letters: *If you have the guts, the stomach . . .* Carefully, she lifted the dome-topped lid and threw the top open.

They all crouched silently, staring into the trunk with wide eyes.

Do we dare open it?

15 THE MAGIC HORSE TRACKS

"Empty!" Michele gasped.

"*Empty*," moaned Brian. "Not even another clue."

Someone was mean and cruel to tease them so, Michele thought. Why hadn't the dumb clue-writer just left them alone, never sent them any notes at all?

Suddenly, they heard footsteps on the back porch as people gathered for the first tour. They slammed the trunk lid closed and dashed downstairs, slipping out the front door just as the back door squeaked open.

The other kids hurried down the walk and out the front gate. But Michele stood on the porch and stared through the window into the hall at the lustre. She had never felt so tricked, so cheated. She thought the mystery would be like a play and all the pieces would fall together for a happy ending.

She glared suspiciously at the tourists filling up the hall. She wouldn't be surprised if the mean old head thief was there in the group laughing at them, knowing they had been there, excited, searching, believing they would find the head and save the play.

She ran her finger over the rough etchings that had been scratched in the windowpanes by the door. Her finger involuntarily traced one name over and over . . . "Ormond . . . Ormond," Michele muttered to herself.

103

The tour guide opened the front door.

"Why, Michele, I didn't know you were out there. Won't you join our tour? You haven't seen this house yet," she said. "There's lots of interesting things here, like the names you were looking at just now." She turned to the group. "When the young ladies of Bath wanted to test their engagement rings they would write their names on the window. If the stone would cut into the glass, they knew it was a real diamond and not a fake stone.

"Here's one," she said, putting her finger beside Michele's. "*Ormond*. That was Blackbeard's wife's maiden name, and the name many of his descendants have used instead of Teach, Blackbeard's real last name."

When the guide led the visitors back inside, Michele turned and fled to catch up with the others.

They were all glum the next morning. Even John was in a bad mood and had ordered the irritable bunch outdoors. They sat sulkily by the water. Just as they had expected, there was another bottle. But even though they could see the note tucked inside, they just let it sit in the dirt and drip. Even Fuzzbucket just sat in the sun and ignored the bottle.

"C'mon," pleaded Michael. "We might as well open it and read the clue."

"That's right," agreed Jo Dee. "We don't even have to do what it says."

"It probably says nanny-nanny-boo-boo, I tricked you," grumbled Michele.

They all giggled in spite of themselves.

Quickly, Michael unstoppered the bottle. Reluctantly, Michele took the note and read:

"You'd better hurry,
Or you'll never get it back;
I've put the head
In the Magic Horse Tracks."

"Oh, no!" Brian and Jo Dee moaned together.

"Oh no *what?*" Michele asked in alarm.

Brian shook his head in dismay. "If he's put the head in the tracks, they'll be gone for sure. We're probably too late now."

"Why?" insisted Michele once more. "What?" Her disinterest had disappeared. She felt like she could shake the answer out of Brian.

Pacing back and forth by the water, Brian explained, "The Magic Horse Tracks are five hoofprints near Washington. Anything put on the tracks disappears and is never seen again."

"Aw c'mon," Michele said, aggravated that Brian would get her so excited over some corny, local hocus-pocus.

Michael had been listening quietly. Michele could see he believed the tale. "Where does the stuff go?" he asked.

"Nobody knows," said Brian. "But they've been there a hundred and fifty years and it's happened every time anything was put there," he added, looking sternly at Michele.

"How did the hoofprints get there?" she asked skeptically.

"The legend says a man named Jesse Elliot was horse racing. He must have had a bet or something, 'cause he shouted to his horse, *Take me in a winner or take me to hell!*"

"You said a bad word," Michael interrupted.

"It's OK when you're quoting someone else, silly," Brian argued. "Anyway," he continued, "when the guy said that, they say the horse took two big leaps and stopped so fast that its hooves dug into the ground. The sudden stop hurled the rider against a tree."

"Ouch!" Michael said, rubbing his head in mock pain.

"More than just *ouch*," said Jo Dee. "It killed him."

"Grass grows all around, but the tracks are smooth and clean," said Brian. "People have put all sorts of things there but they always disappear."

Michele slumped her shoulders and sighed. She didn't want to ask, but . . . "How long does it take for them to disappear?"

Brian paced silently. "Sometimes a couple of days . . . sometimes just a few hours."

Michele jumped up. "Wow! We've got to get over there," she said, ignoring Brian's satisfaction that he had made a believer out of her.

She stuffed the clue in her pocket, tossed the bottle under the deck and raced to keep up with the others who were already heading for their bikes.

Just as they were riding off, John stormed out the back door. He hung over the rail of the deck and waved a wooden spoon at them. "Oh no you don't!" he shouted. "You characters have been disappearing right and left for days. Get in here and eat first."

Michele sighed in relief. "I was afraid he'd been listening to us," she whispered to Brian as they parked their bikes against the boat house.

"Doesn't matter," he grumbled. "We'll be stuck here another hour eating and cleaning up. It's a long ride to Washington. It'll probably be too late when we get there."

In their rush to eat breakfast, Michael sloshed cereal down the front of his tee shirt. Jo Dee spilled her juice. Michele just piddled with her grits and eggs, while Brian gobbled his food like he was in a contest.

"What's with you kids?" John asked impatiently.

No one answered.

"After you clean up the kitchen, I want someone to sweep the deck and walk, someone to feed Tideriggings and the other two to go to the store for me."

"We can't," Michael blurted out.

John narrowed his eyes and peered over his coffee cup at Michael's face turning red as he sunk down in his chair. The others studied the food on their plates like it was a biology assignment.

John spoke, the smoke rising from the hot coffee with each word. "You want to bet you can't?"

He slammed his cup down with a clatter against the saucer and glared at each of them. "I don't know what's going on," he said, "but there are still responsibilities to be taken care of, even if it is summer vacation."

Jo Dee and Michael volunteered to go to the store, in hopes they could spend the change on candy. As soon as Brian and Michele finished their chores, they pedaled as fast as they could across the bridge over Bath Creek and down the straight, hot road toward Washington.

After what seemed like hours to Michele, Brian slowed down, then made a sharp turn off the road into the woods. The dark shade seemed to gobble them up as they disappeared into the trees. Michele blinked her eyes at the sudden change from the glaring sunlight. Then Brian stopped so quickly that she had to grab her hand brakes to keep from plowing into him.

"Hey, you want me to bump my head against a tree, too?" she asked.

Brian had stopped at the edge of a clearing and just stood there staring down at the ground. Michele threw her bike down and ran to the spot. In the opening, just as Brian had described, was the set of strange hoofprints. Grass grew all around, but the marks were as clean as could be. They were also empty. Michele moaned and squatted down beside the prints.

"Maybe the clue was just another joke," Michele said.

"Maybe," said Brian, "but look." He motioned to a clump of bushes. Half hidden under some low branches was a brown canvas sack.

"Didn't anything put on the tracks ever show up again?" she asked hopefully.

"Never," said Brian. "Not ever."

Michele crawled over and tugged at the rope drawstring. The sack pulled away with ease. She picked it up gingerly and looked inside. "It's empty," she said.

"Well I guess that's that," Brian said, standing up and

dusting the sand off of his hands.

"I don't think so," Michele said defiantly. "I still think this clue was a trick too. That ugly bearded man just wanted us to believe the head was truly gone so we wouldn't look anymore."

"Well we've looked all over Bath," Brian grumbled.

"Exactly," agreed Michele. "But from the beginning of this mystery, nothing has been like it seemed to be. It seemed like the head would be in Bath from all the clues — but I don't think it is."

"What do you mean?" asked Brian.

"I think there's a very logical place for Blackbeard's head to be, a place where it would be safe, and that's where we're going right now," Michele said stubbornly, slinging the canvas sack into the biggest of the hoofprints.

16 STRANDED AT PLUM POINT

"Where?" asked Brian.

"Where else would Blackbeard's head be more at home or more difficult to find than the place where he lived — Plum Point!"

By the time they got back to the motel and had rounded up the kids, the sun was going down.

"Hurry up, you guys," urged Brian, herding them to the end of the pier.

Michele was already on the pier, pacing back and forth trying to figure out how they were going to get to Plum Point.

"There's our chance!" she suddenly hollered to the others. "Come on."

Cap'n, who ran the boat dock when he wasn't asleep on the pier with a bottle of beer in his hand, was just pushing off in his dinghy to check his crab pots.

Michele decided he didn't know much about kids or he would have asked them if they had permission to head out to sea at dusk. Of course it was hard for them to ask John when he had gone to Belhaven to pick up some people who had come over on the ferry from Ocracoke to see the play.

They clambered aboard the rickety boat. Brian sat in the

bow. Michele nervously noted the couple of inches of water sloshing abound in the bottom of the craft. The water slithered in and out of Jo Dee's flip flops with the rocking motion. Michael held tightly to the sides.

They bobbed precariously through the gray waves in silence. The farther away from the shore they got, the more Michele's stomach felt like she had swallowed a bottle of glue and all her insides were stuck together in one big blob.

Here they were in a seaworn, instead of seaworthy boat. They had no lifejackets and were sailing with a man who smelled strongly of alcohol. They didn't know exactly where they were going, what would happen when they got there, and how or even if they would get back.

After a while Brian pointed to the narrow strip of land jutting out into the bay and shouted, "There's Plum Point, Cap'n."

"You kids 'spect you're going to find some bur'd treasure," Cap'n slurred. "But I 'spect it's all slipslidin' around in the tunnel old Blackie Beard built 'neath the sea 'tween Plumy Point and the Guv'ners place on Archbell Point." He slung his arm toward the land directly across the bay.

"No one could build an underwater tunnel that far," Brian argued.

"It wasn't that far, back then, sonny. The points were much closer before the years and the tides took their toll. Eroded, they have. Shiftin' sand. That's what's made these waters so treacherous for centuries."

"Well, we're looking for a different treasure . . ." Brian began, then stopped.

"New treasure, 'eh?" Cap'n sounded interested. They

surely didn't need him to stick around, Michele thought. But he muttered some words to himself that Michele hoped the kids didn't hear, and seemed to forget his interest in them or their treasure.

They drifted toward the bobbing crabpot markers and away from the sandy, curved shore of Plum Point.

"That way, sir," Brian reminded the old man.

"Right sonny," Cap'n said and swung the boat about so sharply that they almost fell into the water.

They hit the shore with a thud. Michael tumbled out of the boat, slipped and fell bottom first into the surf.

"I'm wet," he moaned, salty tears streaming from his eyes. He crawled up on the beach and put his head on his arms.

Jo Dee climbed out next, holding her stomach.

"You feel sick?" Michele asked.

"Seasick," Jo Dee whispered hoarsely through clenched teeth. She waded through the water and laid down on the sand.

"Here, sonny," Cap'n said, shoving a busted oar at Brian. "T'will protect you from the snakes and spooks. I'll be back 'fore dark-thirty."

"Thanks sir," Brian said. He jumped overboard and marched directly ahead into the green jungle.

Cap'n has forgotten our problems, Michele thought. All he has on his mind is treasure.

Michele plopped down on the wet sand between the two kids. Mumbling under his breath again, Cap'n pushed off. It was quiet except for Michael's muffled sobbing, Jo Dee's labored breathing, and the plip-plop of the waves against the lonesome stretch of beach.

Michele craned her neck to look behind her. Brian had disappeared into the tall, thick strands of sea oats. It was spooky on the beach with the sunset shadows gobbling up the green woods behind her. Out in the sound, dark storm clouds that she hadn't noticed before grew fatter and darker by the minute.

It had seemed like the right thing to come here, Michele thought. But it had seemed the right thing to do everything. All had led to dead ends, and this seemed the deadest of all.

Michele felt miserable. She wished she could either cry like Michael or just cover her head like Jo Dee. She had truly lost her head, and maybe more, over this mystery.

Suddenly, she jumped up and waved frantically toward the boat vanishing in the twilight. *Dark thirty?* She doubted Cap'n would even remember he had brought them, much less to pick them up. And no one, *no one* knew they were here on this uninhabited island in the Graveyard of the Atlantic.

"Cap'n, come back!" she cried. Her words were lost in the threatening wind. The old man looked up once and she hollered again. But he just waved, and she figured he thought she was saying good-bye. And she probably was — forever.

She sat down in the cold, wet sand.

It really is too late, Michele thought. Because of all of the unfortunate incidents, the final performance of the play would begin almost anytime.

From her pockets, Michele pulled out the clues that had kept them running in circles all summer. She plastered them in the wet sand. The ragged edges of the torn paper seemed to melt together.

Suddenly, she realized they were melting together in a pattern. It was a map! Not a treasure map, but a map of Bath — like you could get at the Historic Center.

She shifted the pieces until their edges touched one another. Each piece made up a location where they had searched unsuccessfully for the head.

Only one place was not marked. Only one place where they had not been directed to look. A place where they could not even look now — not as long as they were stranded at Plum Point.

"Brian! Brian!" Michele screamed into the dark jungle of green behind her.

17 At Sea In A Storm

Holding her stomach with one hand, Jo Dee propped herself up to see what Michele was hollering about.

Brian streaked out of the woods, the oar raised menacingly over his head. He looked like a pirate was chasing him.

"Snake?" he asked.

"No, yuck!" Michele said. "Look! Look . . . the clues make up a map!"

"Treasure?" asked Brian hopefully.

"No, a map of Bath. See, each clue we found led us to a different site in town. None were right. Least of all this place," she said, fearfully eyeing the advancing storm.

"There's only one place we haven't really looked for the head," Michele said. She pointed to a corner of the map. "Catnip Point!"

"But that's where the amphitheater is," Brian said. "The head couldn't be there or someone would have found it a long time ago. Besides, we did look there once, when we were going to make a new head."

"Yes — but we were looking for cloth, not a head," explained Michele. "Of course, whoever slammed the prop room door and scared us didn't know that."

"You mean they thought we were looking for the missing head?" Brian asked.

"Of course," said Michele. "And we must have been close. That's why they've been leading us on this wild goose, or rather, *head* chase. They made us look all over town. Michele pointed down to the soggy, jigsaw map again. "All the clues were written to keep us away from the play site. It seemed like the head would not be there for sure. But everything that has seemed one way all summer has been just the opposite. I know the head is there somewhere, and we've got to get back and fast. The play must be through the first act by now."

"Look Michele," Brian said, angrily. "I'm tired of looking for this head. I don't care about being in any old play. I'd rather find some real treasure. Besides that, how are we going to get back before the play ends? It's impossible. Mr. Tankard will just have to announce like he planned that this is the last performance and season. If they find the head later, well, somebody can just use it on Halloween to scare little kids or something."

"Hush Brian," Michele cautioned. She could tell the younger kids were really scared. The storm was almost upon them. Pink lightning flickered in the blue–black clouds.

"This is a dangerous place to be during an electrical storm," Michele said. "There's no place to go for protection."

"Look!" said Brian. "A boat."

In the dim twilight, a small rowboat was approaching the shore. Each wave seemed to toss it toward them. A head became visible. It was a man – the man with the black beard!

Now it was Michele's turn to feel sick and near tears. It had been him all along, she thought. He led them to a pirate's island in the storm at dark with no way to escape. And now he was coming to get them.

Jo Dee and Michael sat very still in the sand. Brian clutched the splintered oar and moved protectively in front of them.

Michele felt glued to the wet beach. The salt in the blowing wind stung her eyes, yet she continued to stare at the small boat moving threateningly toward them. She thought she would give almost anything for the four of them to be back at the motel playing Monopoly on the bed and watching TV and eating potato chips and dip.

The man kept his face lowered against the wind. His wet and matted black curls twitched with each gust. As the boat bumped the shore a few feet from them, he slowly lifted his head and squinted at them.

"This is no place to be in a squall," he said. "Where's your craft? I'll bet your parents are worried about you."

For a few minutes the kids sat as still as sandcastles.

The man climbed out quickly and came toward Brian. He reached for the splintered oar. For a second, as Michele held her breath tightly, Brian and the man both gripped the oar. Then Brian let his hand fall slowly away.

"We got a ride out to explore," Michele explained, her voice rising and falling in the tumultuous air. "Cap'n is coming back for us soon."

With his feet planted wide in the sand for balance, his hands perched on his hips and his head tossed back in the wind, curls flying, the man towered over them. But his sudden laughter sounded friendly, not evil.

He reached down to help Jo Dee to her feet. "Not likely," he said. "I just passed Cap'n anchored at Archbell Point. I imagine he's snoring away right now, sleeping out the storm.

You'd better come back to Bath with me. It can be right spooky here at night when the moon is out, much less in a snarling storm."

"Have you spent the night on Plum Point before?" Brian asked, suspiciously.

"Sure, some college buddies of mine came down one weekend and we brought our sleeping bags out here. One of them told us a lot of good pirate stories. I'm afraid we were lazy and didn't even look for treasure. I do enough digging all day as it is."

Visions of gravediggers ran through Michele's mind.

"Dig?" she repeated.

"Yes. My name is Ray Whitley. I'm an archaeologist. I've seen you kids around town when I was coming back in after a digging expedition. That'll make you dirty and tired, especially lugging all my tools around half the night."

"In a brown bag?" asked Michele.

"Yes," he answered, looking at her as though he were very puzzled at the question.

"Why did you come to Plum Point tonight?" Michele asked, still suspicious.

"The man I rent a room from wasn't feeling well. I offered to check his crab pots," he said, nodding toward his boat which was floundering in the tumbling waves.

"Will you take us home?" asked Jo Dee with a shaky voice.

"Please!" echoed Michael, wincing at lightning that darted in and out of the clouds like the silvery jumping mullet did in the water by the motel.

A sudden silver streak hit behind them and no one even hesitated to wait for the man's answer. Hastening to the boat,

Ray and Brian helped Michael and Jo Dee inside.

As Michele lifted one bare-toed foot over the side she squealed. A crab had escaped from one of the pots and was scurrying around the bottom of the boat. "Super choice," she said to Brian. "Stranded on a pirate island or eaten alive by a crab."

The lightning crackled again and no one laughed at Michele's joke. As Ray headed the boat into the wind, they bumped and bounced, gripping the sides of the boat tightly. Ray motioned for Michele to pass out the life jackets, then he turned grim-faced to the task of maneuvering the little craft towards Bath.

The lightning bounced in psychedelic streaks on the water before them. The foamy spray spewed them with a salty sting. Michele tucked her feet tightly under her. Jo Dee clung to one side of her, Michael to the other. Michele felt proud of Brian who used the flimsy, splintered oar in an effort to help Ray who was beginning to look exhausted.

A final lunge of oars and bolt of lightning seemed to thrust them into view of the harbor.

"We're almost there!" cried Michael. Jo Dee clenched her lips tightly and did not speak.

Michele was relieved to see the storm was veering off toward Archbell Point. Poor Cap'n. Of course, he did forget us, she thought.

As the boat shifted to a slower pace, Michele sighed with relief. She squinted at the shore, watching for the glow of the theater, "I don't see any lights," she told Brian.

They both stretched and craned their necks like the turtles

in Bath Creek, but the sky above Catnip Point looked dark without even any freckles of stars or its usual smile of a moon.

"Land Ho!" cried Ray as they thudded to a stop against the pier.

Michele's palms hurt as she unclenched her hands.

"I'll help Jo Dee," said Ray.

"Watch the crabby crab," Michael warned as Michele tumbled out almost face first in her haste.

She knew they should thank Ray and invite him in for some coffee and to put on some of John's dry clothes if he wanted to.

But a close glimpse of Bath revealed to Michele what she had feared. It had already rained here — and hard. The tall grass near shore glistened with raindrops and the uneven boards of the dock were puddled.

They didn't bother to explain to Ray about the mystery and how they had thought he was the one who had caused so much trouble. Michele just couldn't think of a way to explain all that fast enough.

So, with a mumble of "thank you's" and "play," they hustled Jo Dee and Michael through the wet bushes toward the theater.

"*Play?*" Ray called after them in a baffled voice. "Is that all you kids think about — playing?"

"We'll explain later," Michele called back, feeling rude to run off and leave someone who had rescued them.

As they scampered up the wet, slippery hill, she confessed her fear to Brian. "I think the play's been rained out — and our last chance at solving the mystery is all washed up!"

18 STAGEFRIGHT!

When they reached the theater, Mr. Tankard greeted them grouchily. "The rain's stopped just in time. Full house tonight, kids. Do you know what evil eyes I've gotten trying to save four seats on the front row for you? Where in the world have you been?"

The four of them coughed and stuttered and mumbled at him.

"Oh, tell me later," he said exasperatedly. "I've got to get backstage. If we can just make it through tonight, it will be good-bye and good riddance. I give up kids, I just give up. I'm afraid this will be the final curtain on our outdoor drama dream."

Michele watched Tank walk away, his shoulders slumped dejectedly. He was right, she thought. The play was entering its final act of its final performance of its final run. She knew the head was here. The real villain was probably here too, smirking at them in the darkness. And there was just no way to figure it all out fast enough to save the play.

The other kids slipped down the dark aisle to their seats. Michele followed and sat down exhaustedly beside them. Jo Dee handed her a program. Michael stuffed a fistful of popcorn into a yawn. How could he eat at a time like this, Michele wondered.

Jo Dee nudged Michele. "Doesn't Susan look pretty?" she asked.

The actress did look lovely as Mary Ormond, Blackbeard's wife, Michele thought. She couldn't seem to help feeling envious of Susan's opportunity to be in a real play.

"Hey," Jo Dee whispered. "Susan's not acting — she's crying real tears."

"She knows this is the end of the play," Michele said. She looked down and pretended she was reading the program as her own eyes blurred with tears. Some mystery solver I am, she thought. All summer — and no better off than when we started. Now the only mystery will be *the missing play mystery.* We'll know where it went, but not really why. And it'll be years before I see my name in a program like this, she thought, blinking away her tears and reading the names of the cast and crew.

"Like this!" she said suddenly in a loud whisper.

"Sssh," muttered a woman behind them.

Michele pointed to a name on the program with her finger then turned and punched Brian in the ribs. "I know who did it!" she said.

"You're crazy," said Brian.

Michele glared at him.

The last scene was already underway. They were pulling down the back of the stage to expose the *Adventurer*, the ship Blackbeard sailed to his final battle at Teach's Hole. In just seconds the gun blast would begin. Blackbeard would be decapitated once more and a forlorn actor–pirate would hold up a cardboard sword instead of the gruesome head that had been specially designed for the play. Michele couldn't believe that a head she had never even seen before could cause her so much trouble.

Pointing over and over to a name in the program, Michele whispered loudly and hurriedly to Brian. In disbelief, he nodded understandingly at her. The pinkish-red blast flared in the dark. Sword clanked sword and booted feet clomped on the dark deck of the ship.

Even though she knew who had stolen the head Michele still didn't know why. But she did know what she had to do now. She had to go on the stage, stop the play, and tell everyone. Now or never. It was her cue.

Suddenly, the very thing she had dreamed about for years and had always wanted so badly seemed like the most awful thing in the world. Butterflies belted the inside of her stomach. Her knees and elbows felt like jellyfish. It was an acute attack of stagefright, worse that she could have ever imagined. But she knew the show must go on, so the drama could go on again and again.

Suddenly she realized how actors and actresses overcame that sickening fear that attacks the most experienced of them the moment before their feet hit the stage and the lights flood their face — they just do it. They make themselves move. They must. The cast who has worked so hard, the audience who has come so expectantly, are counting on them.

And they just go on.

Michele gave Michael and Jo Dee the skull and

crossbones sign, then said to Brian, "We're on!"

As if there weren't enough chaos on stage with a full–fledged pirate battle going on, they both rushed to the stage, Michele in one direction, Brian another.

19 THE HEAD IN HER HANDS

Michele never felt her feet touch the stage steps. "There, Mr. Tankard, there!" she shouted. The play manager ran onstage looking as mad as a pirate. The audience hummed in confusion.

As Brian lunged across the stage, the darkness zoomed to daylight as the house lights went up. The actor playing Blackbeard, supposedly dead in the play, appeared with his hands on his hips looking fiercer than the real Ned Teach. Other cast members stormed out of the wings. Everyone froze in place. Michele felt the angry, questioning eyes of the cast and crew on her and Brian, wondering what they were doing and why they would ruin what might be the final performance of the play like this.

"It's him," Michele shouted, pointing toward the wings. "*He* has the head."

On the edge of the stage, trying to hide from the floodlights was Ozzie Ormond, alias Oswald Teach, clutching the replica of Blackbeard's head. The missing head was found!

"You have some center stage explaining to do young lady," Tank said.

Michele turned to assure him that she and Brian weren't the ones up to no good, but he just waved the script back and forth between her and the audience and said, "Tell *them!*

They are the ones who have paid to see the drama. Not part of it, not the end messed up, not kids romping on stage during the climax. Tell them!"

Now it was Michele's turn to freeze. Suddenly, she was truly on center stage. She took one small step forward toward the audience and thought that with all these people around she had never felt more alone or afraid. She had never realized that you couldn't see the audience with the lights shining in your face. And she could feel the eyes of the audience on her even though she could not actually see their questioning gazes.

"Um," she said softly, then realized that would never do. She cleared her throat and spoke louder. "I'm really sorry about messing up the end of the play you came to see," she began.

"Even if you didn't see the end of the play, you probably know Blackbeard lost his head in a battle at Teach's Hole near Ocracoke. Well, the head that was supposed to be Blackbeard's was stolen from the prop room earlier this summer. A lot of other bad things happened after that too and now there won't be a play.

"And this man over here," Michele pointed to Ormond, "well he . . . he . . ." she couldn't go on. But the show must always go on, she thought. But she couldn't tell on Ormond in front of all these people. Maybe he had some reason for stealing the head. He looked so scared, cowering there in the exit. Maybe she was mistaken.

But now he was coming toward her with the ugly head in his hands.

"Yes," he said, looking more scared than scary. "I took the head. Many years ago I had a successful business in Bath. I had a lovely wife. And I had a heritage, for Blackbeard is my ancestor. As this young girl must have figured out, many of the Teach descendants took the name of Ormond, Blackbeard's wife's maiden name.

"I was happy and prosperous here. Then the main road through Bath was moved and my business began to fail. I went bankrupt. My beautiful wife, Memory, loved Bath and the historic homes. We used to sit together each evening and look out at Plum Point. But after I lost my shop, we lost our home too. We moved to Washington so I could work. Memory missed Bath so much. She drove back every week just to wander around the historic district. Late one afternoon on her way to Bath, she was killed in an auto accident on the new highway. If she had lived, she probably would have played the part of Blackbeard's wife in the play. She was that beautiful," he added, near tears.

"Now, I'm ashamed to admit that because I work for the costumer, I had access to the head and hid it. I was hurt and angry at the people who were coming to see Bath when Memory couldn't anymore. I thought they were intruders on my heritage. But I see they love Bath too and only want to share it for awhile. I was wrong and selfish and hurt them and Memory's beloved Bath."

Michele didn't think she was allowed to cry on center stage — or scream which she thought about as Ormond handed her the ugly head.

"Here, forgive me," he pleaded. "Hang my own head from

a bowsprit of a ship, but let the play go on."

Everyone in the cast looked at Mr. Tankard. His own head hung down as he stared at the planks of the stage. The hot lights made Michele's skin sweat and mosquitoes attacked the back of her neck. You can't even scratch on center stage, she thought.

Finally, the play manager looked up. "Bath belongs to us," he said. "But the heritage and history of the Albemarle region belong to everyone and we must share it."

He looked at Ormond and sighed, "Yes, the play will go on — thanks to Michele and her friends' solution to the problems we've encountered this summer."

Michele had turned to Tank to hear his decision. But now behind her she heard a strange, muffled sound that grew louder, then louder in her ears. It was applause! The audience was on its feet clapping, whistling, stamping their feet. Even the cast joined in. Michele was so happy, she hugged the ugly head.

Mr. Tankard came up to Michele and handed her his script. "You'd better memorize this, young lady."

"You mean I can try out for the play next year?"

"No. I mean you'd better show up for rehearsals as soon as school's out next spring. You'll make a good actress. At least, you put on quite a performance tonight!"

Blackbeard's head is found!

20 APPLAUSE!

The next morning Michele stood in front of the Harbor Motel and took a final look across the bay. The air was almost cool. Michele guessed it must be the first hint of autumn and school.

"Here, I'll take that," Brian said, grabbing the box of shells Michele was supposed to be loading in the car to take back home to Raleigh. Brian was being brusque, but Michele believed he would miss her as much as she was going to miss him and Jo Dee – and Bath.

And John, she thought, as he patted her shoulder on his way from the car to get another load of suitcases. She was sure going to miss him and his good cooking.

She grabbed his arm as he went by. "John, you will come to see us in Raleigh, won't you?" she asked.

"Of course," he said. "And I'll bring my recipe for crab crepes along."

"Yum," said Michele. "Will you bring Brian and Jo Dee too?"

"Of course!" he repeated. "We'll come for your first school theatrical production . . . or rather your second, after last night!"

The very thought made Michele tingle all over. She reached back and patted her jean pocket to make sure the envelope was still there. Mr. Tankard had given her a letter stating she was scheduled to appear in the outdoor drama next season. It was on his theater stationery and looked very official. She was sure that would be proof of her so-called "interest and ability" and should ensure her a place in the drama club this year. She must have read a hundred times the sentence that said, "Without Michele's dedication to the theater, our historic drama would not have even continued to exist."

John stopped beside her on his trip back to the car and rapped her gently on the top of her head with his knuckles. "You in there?" he asked.

Michele blushed, realizing she'd been standing in the middle of all the packing commotion daydreaming. "Oh John, I don't think I can wait until next summer comes!"

Michael had been tearing around the yard waving his now raggedy pirate flag. "No more bottles to wash up to the shore," he moaned.

"Well you never know," said John. "You were so busy with this mystery that you didn't even get to search for Blackbeard's treasure."

"Hey that's right," Brian said. "If we'd solved the missing treasure mystery instead of the missing head mystery, you could have bought yourself Broadway and been in any play you wanted to," he said to Michele.

They all laughed.

"And nobody wanted to come to Bath," reminded Mother. "It was going to be an awful, terrible, boring summer," she teased.

Michele blushed again and hugged her Mother. "Things

aren't always what they seem," she said. That made her think of Ozzie Ormond. "What will happen to Mr. Ormond?" she asked John.

"Yeah, that meanie," said Jo Dee.

"I don't think you understand," said Mother. "The man didn't really mean any harm to anyone personally. I guess he just felt frustrated about things happening one way when he thought they should be another."

"Of course, he didn't know four kids were going to show up and show off their detective skills," said John.

"Even when they weren't supposed to," Mother added and Michele was relieved to see she was smiling.

"I guess he had to resort to things like clues in bottles and scaring us in the churchyard to keep us away from the amphitheater," Brian added.

"And there the head was all the time, under a false bottom of the trunk in the prop room."

"I still don't see how you knew who had done it," Mother said.

"Well, the Bonner House guide told me about the Teach's using the Ormond name. So when I saw Ormond in the program as costumer's assistant, I thought he might really be a Teach, like in pirate," Michele explained.

"And we had seen a man at the amphitheater dressed as a pirate — the same day the prop room keys disappeared," Brian said.

"Yeah," moaned Michele, "The same day we were looking in the trunk where the head was!"

Mother gave John a stern look.

"And you saw another pirate in the graveyard that night," said Jo Dee.

Now Mother really glared at John who looked like he wondered if these were the same kids who had stayed with him all summer.

They all grinned at John and giggled.

"Things aren't what they seem to be," John assured Mother.

"I'm sure glad," said Michele, thinking how wrong they'd been about poor Ray. She was glad he'd followed them to the play that night and so had understood what was going on. He had even come back to the Harbor Light with them for a late supper and celebration. That's when he had told them about his investigation of the Magic Horse Tracks and leaving one of his canvas sample sacks behind. No wonder there had not been a clue in it, Michele thought.

"Well," said John, "Since Ormond did return everything he took and agreed to make two new heads for next year's performance, I don't think they'll be too hard on him. After all, this mess has helped show us all how much the past, present, *and future* of Bath mean to everyone."

Suddenly, the chattering grew quiet and Michele felt sad that summer really was over.

"Bath," said Mother.

"It's a pretty place," said Michele looking wistfully out at the calm bay where they had enjoyed so many nice swims. Now Fuzzbucket would have it all to himself.

"I don't mean the city Bath," corrected Mother. "This time I mean a real bath with soap and water," she said, running her fingers through Michael's hair. "That's what you're both going to take as soon as we get home."

"Yuck!" said Michael, swatting his flag on the ground. "I'm clean from going swimming."

Finally, they climbed in the crowded car. John stuck his head in the window and kissed Mother. Next he kissed Michele on the cheek. "Star!" he said and Michele kissed him back. He shook Michael's hand heartily and said, "Ye been a fine first mate, me man. Ye can sail aboard me ship any summer!"

As Mother headed the car for the highway, she said, "You two sure got quiet in the back seat. I thought you'd be telling Jo Dee and Brian good-bye all the way across the bridge."

Michele and Michael giggled. "We are," they said, as they perched on their knees facing out the back window. They each gave the skull and crossbones sign and Jo Dee and Brian returned it.

When they crossed the bridge over the bay, Michele waved good–bye to Catnip Point and the mast of the *Adventurer* sticking up into the sky.

Then she snuggled back into the seat against a stack of beach towels. As she closed her eyes to dream about being in the play next summer, the water slap–slapping beneath the bridge sounded to her like a sea of applause.

The End

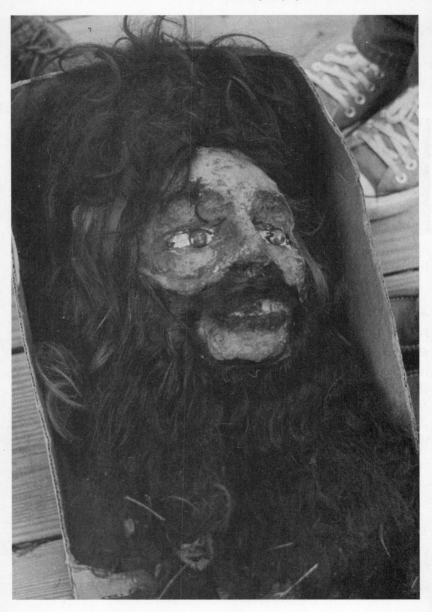

ABOUT THE AUTHOR

Carole Marsh is an author and publisher who has written many works of fiction and non-fiction for young readers. She travels throughout the United States and around the world to research her books. In 1979 Carole Marsh was named Communicator of the Year for her corporate communications work with major national and international corporations.

Marsh is the founder and CEO of Gallopade International, established in 1979. Today, Gallopade International is widely recognized as a leading source of educational materials for every state and many countries. Marsh and Gallopade were recipients of the 2002 Teachers' Choice Award. Marsh has written more than 13 Carole Marsh Mysteries™. Years ago, her children, Michele and Michael, were the original characters in her mystery books. Today, they continue the Carole Marsh Books tradition by working at Gallopade. By adding grandchildren Grant and Christina as new mystery characters, she has continued the tradition for a third generation.

Ms. Marsh welcomes correspondence from her readers. You can e-mail her at carole@gallopade.com, visit the carolemarshmysteries.com website, or write to her in care of Gallopade International, P.O. Box 2779, Peachtree City, Georgia, 30269 USA.

Built-In Book Club
Talk About It!

1. Who was your favorite character? Why?

2. What was your favorite part of the book? Why?

3. Do you like to read stories about pirates?
   Why or why not?

4. When the author described Blackbeard's head, were
   you able to picture it in your mind? Talk about how
   we all visualize things in our mind every day, in many
   situations.

5. What was the scariest thing that happened in the
   book?

6. Would you ever want to live the life of a pirate? What
   would be good about it, and what would be not-so-
   good?

7. How do pirates of the past compare to the
   terrorists of today? How are
   piracy and terrorism similar
   and different?

8. Did you miss the characters
   when you finished the book?
   What do you think they
   might do next?

Built-In Book Club
Bring It To Life!

1. Make a pirate ship! The whole book club group can work together on this project. First, get a big box from a place that sells appliances. Paint your ship, write the name on the side, and add blue waves crashing against your ship. You might want to put some angry sharks in the water! Then, add a pirate flag (a broomstick handle and a piece cut from an old sheet will work) and a treasure chest full of coins made from aluminum foil or construction paper. Ahoy, Mates!

2. Have a pirate party! Wear pirate hats, striped shirts, shorts, and of course, an eye patch! Serve some punch as your "grog," and decorate cupcakes with "treasures"— like small candy pieces or sprinkles. Make up names for each other like "One-legged Larry," or "Belinda Bones!" Play some games like "Swab the Deck," where two pirates compete to see who can sweep five lively ping-pong balls across the room first! AAAAAARRRRRRGGGGGHHHHH!

3. Do the math! Break the club into small groups to tackle a "piratical" math problem! If gold sells for $250 per ounce, and Blackbeard's treasure totaled 25 pounds of gold, how much money would you have if you found his buried loot? If you had to pay 40 percent tax on this treasure, what would you have left to keep?

GLOSSARY

bandolier: a broad belt worn over the shoulder by pirates that has small pockets used to store pistols

bow: the front end of a ship or boat

bowsprit: a small pole, sometimes used to support a figurehead, that projects out from the bow of the ship over the water

buccaneer: another name for a pirate

cutlass: a short and heavy sword that is slightly curved

dastardly: cowardly or sneaky

decapitate: to remove someone's head by force

grog: a strong drink made from alcohol mixed with water

hardtack: a hard biscuit made without salt that could keep for long periods of time

loot: anything stolen by force or secrecy

plunder: to steal things from other people by force

ransack: to aggressively search for valuable plunder

stern: the back end of a ship or boat

swashbuckler: a swaggering adventurer or daredevil

yardarm: the outer end of a spar that hangs a square sail

Pirate's Scavenger Hunt!

Recipe for fun: Read the book, take the tour, find the items on this list and check them off! (Hint: Look high and low!!) *Teachers: you have permission to reproduce this form for your students.*

__1. Historic Center

__2. St. Thomas Church

__3. Palmer-Marsh House

__4. twin chimneys

__5. a duck

__6. a dog

__7. a tombstone

__8. a skull and crossbones

__9. a historic marker

__10. the word "Bath"

BLACKBEARD'S EXPLOITS

Blackbeard and the crew of his Queen Anne's Revenge really got around! During the Golden Age of Piracy they looted, plundered, ransacked, and generally made pests of themselves from Maine to Florida. Here are just a few of their dastardly exploits:

• Off the coast of New England, Blackbeard set afire sulfur matches behind his ears, and in the fog looked so fearsome that most ships under attack immediately surrendered rather than fight!

• Citizens of Charles Towne (Charleston), South Carolina were horror-stricken to learn that Blackbeard's ship was offshore and ready to shoot its cannon unless medicine and other supplies were rowed out to the pirates!

• Blackbeard often careened (overturned) his ship in Virginia's waters to scrape barnacles from the bottom so they could speed even faster after their prey!

FROM MAINE TO KEY WEST!

- The *Queen Anne's Revenge* could often be seen ashore a North Carolina sandbar as Blackbeard and his men celebrated a Saturnalia, sort of a holiday party and feast of boucan (the word we get buccaneer and barbecue from!).

- Off the coast of Maryland, Blackbeard intentionally ran his ship aground to trick other pirates in thinking he was stuck . . . when he was really loading treasure aboard!

- It is said that Philadelphia was Blackbeard's favorite place to go to have his large, black, handsome pirate outfits custom made!

- In Bath Town, North Carolina, Blackbeard married his 13th wife, a 13-year-old!

WRITE YOUR OWN MYSTERY!

Make up a dramatic title!

You can pick four real kid characters!

Select a real place for the story's setting!

Try writing your first draft!

Edit your first draft!

Read your final draft aloud!

You can add art, photos or illustrations!

Share your book with others and send me a copy!

SIX SECRET WRITING TIPS FROM CAROLE MARSH!

Enjoy this exciting excerpt from

THE MYSTERY OF THE ALAMO GHOST

1 ALAMO, HERE WE GO!

Mimi wrote kid's books, mysteries mostly, and often used her grandkids (and neighbors' kids, and kids who read her books, and most anyone else between ages 7 and 14 she could get her hands on) as "real" characters in her books. Then she set the story of the book in a real location. This time, it was the Alamo. They were on their way to San Antonio, Texas. And, if they didn't hurry up, they were going to miss their plane.

"Get along little doggies!" Papa shouted, urging them all to move faster toward the train that would take them to Gate 13. Papa always sounded like a cowboy. His business card even had Trail Boss on it as his title.

"Arf! Arf! ARF!! ARF!!!" Grant barked, now poised like a galloping puppy. Great, thought Christina—some people have a brother; I have a dino dog.

"Whoopie-kai-yai-yea!" hollered Papa as the train doors swooshed open and gobbled them inside. Everyone grabbed a pole to hold onto to keep their footing as the train roared off.

"Uh, Mimi . . ." Christina said, giving her grandmother "the look."

"What?" asked Mimi, then looked down and realized her colorful Cirque-du-Soleil umbrella was poking Christina in the stomach. "Oh, sorry."

"I don't need a new bellybutton," Christina said.

"Oh, why not?" said Mimi, gently poking the rounded point of the umbrella in strategic spots where she knew her granddaughter was especially ticklish. Christina tried to grab and cover all those spots at once, while laughing so hard a tear formed in the corner of her eye.

"Why do you have all that rain gear, anyway, Mimi?" she asked. "Papa says it's going to be 101 degrees in San Antonio. I don't think it's gonna rain there."

"You never know," Mimi said. Of course, that's what Mimi always said. Christina guessed that was her mystery state of mind. She recognized that absent-minded look her grandmother always got as she headed toward her next mystery book site. Christina knew that she was always writing in her head. The weird thing was that some of the things her grandmother/writer made up often came true. That, to Christina, was pretty strange and scary. What, she wondered, would happen on this mystery trip adventure? Last time, when Mimi was writing a mystery book during the Boston Marathon, their runner/schoolteacher/cousin Priscilla was kidnapped off the racecourse—right in front of their eyes!

Suddenly, the train stopped and spit them out right at the escalator. "Run!" cried Papa, checking his watch. They all dashed up the escalator and ran toward Gate 13. Everyone was boarding, and they were even calling stand-bys to give them any leftover seats.

"I hope they don't give our seats away," Christina worried aloud.

"Aw, don't worry," Grant said. "You can have my seat. I'll ride up front in the cockpit. In fact, the pilot can have my seat. I'll sit in his and fly us to San Antonio." Grant now took on the pose of an airplane and zoomed around the waiting area as Papa checked them in.

"And we'd end up in Timbuktu," said Christina.

"Yeah, Tim Buck can go too," Grant said.

"Grant, you're incorrigible!" his sister said.

That stopped her brother cold. He froze in his airplane pose, arms outstretched. "Incorrigible? Incorrigible? Hey, that sounds like a compliment to me," he said.

Christina gave him her famous "look" that meant get-off-my-case-leave-me-alone-don't-be-so-stupid-I-don't-know-you-I-am-not-with-these-people-never-seen-them-before. Then she stared at the ceiling.

"Uh, Christina?" Papa said gently. "Going with us?"

Christina looked up and blushed. She realized she had been standing there daydreaming while everyone had boarded but her and Papa. "Uh, sure," she said, ducking past the gate agent and lugging her purple backpack down the corridor to the airplane. As she crossed the threshold over that creepy place where the airplane doesn't quite meet the ramp—where you can see the ground below and air swishes all around you—Christina noted the number of the airplane: 1313. She quickly jumped inside the aircraft and handed the flight attendant her seat pass. The woman smiled at her. "Your row is number 13," she said merrily, pointing the way.

Christina felt the tiny hairs on her arms and neck stand up like little soldiers. Goosebumps formed beneath them. Of course, her row *would* be "lucky" number 13, she thought.

WOULD YOU MYSTERIES LIKE TO BE
A CHARACTER IN A CAROLE MARSH MYSTERY?

If you would like to star in a Carole Marsh Mystery, fill out the form below and write a 25-word paragraph about why you think you would make a good character! Once you're done, ask your mom or dad to send this page to:

Carole Marsh Mysteries Fan Club
Gallopade International
P.O. Box 2779
Peachtree City, GA 30269

My name is: _____

I am a: ____boy _____ girl   Age: _____

I live at: _____

City: _____

State:_____   Zip code: _____

My e-mail address: _____

My phone number is: _____

_____

_____

_____

_____

_____

_____

_____

_____

VISIT THE CAROLE MARSH MYSTERIES WEBSITE

www.carolemarshmysteries.com

- *Check out what's coming up next! Are we coming to your area with our next book release? Maybe you can have your book signed by the author!*

- *Join the Carole Marsh Mysteries Fan Club!*

- *Apply for the chance to be a character in an upcoming Carole Marsh Mystery!*

- *Learn how to write your own mystery!*